DRAGON MY HEART AROUND

DRAGON MY HEART AROUND

PROVIDENCE PARANORMAL COLLEGE BOOK FOUR

D.R. PERRY

CHAPTER ONE

Blaine

I couldn't sleep again. Wondering when the Extramagus would come and try to kill me was an extra pain in my tail. I managed a brash attitude while awake, but my dreams were filled with a shadowy figure force-choking me harder than Vader on a bad day. That sucked big time because I couldn't even watch Episode IV to take my mind off all of it. I just freaked out and shut it off instead, and I loved that movie. That Magi-supremacist bastard should get himself served extra-crispy for ruining my enjoyment of Star Wars. Getting the jump on someone that powerful was light-years above my pay grade, though.

Like I'd done for the first two nights of my Spring Break, I wandered the manse expanse. As I snorted about my rhyme time, that I was a poet and didn't even know it, the worst thing in the world happened. The alarm went off, first the one for the vault and then the hoard inside it.

Why in the nest of the first Broodmother did my mother and

her dandified Air dragon husband have to be at a charity ball? Why had I been such a recluse and refused Bobby's offer to stay with me over Spring Break? Why hadn't I invited all of Tinfoil Hat over for a Poker night? Why weren't my legs moving? I'd frozen when I should have dashed. It was time to make like Queen Elsa and let it go so I could see what the problem was.

I sprinted down the dragon-wide hallway, remembering my nanny Zyra, and how she used to read me Robert Asprin's old *Myth* series. Skeeve's dragon, Gleep, had galloped down hallways toward the bad guys. So had I, as a kid, when the bad guys were pretend. Time to run straight into the danger, just like that stupid fictional dragon. Gleep did it out of loyalty. I did it because Mother would slay me herself if I didn't.

As I ran, I thought about shifting. My dragon slept. He didn't do insomnia, apparently. Once I unsealed the hoard trinket room, I was glad of that. The first thing I saw when I opened the door was a shapely set of legs. I ogled them, then smacked my face with my palm. I'd been a dunderhead, assuming the Extramagus was a guy who'd just send guys.

The itch of my skin going scaly as I started shifting almost distracted me from the woman's face as she turned around, her eyes wide. Once I did, it was hard not to look at her. She had perfect beige skin and melting amber eyes. I'd seen her somewhere before, and she was way too young to be the Extramagus. Besides, she smelled like a shifter. I dialed back on dragoning out, lulling the beast inside back to sleep. A petite Japanese girl couldn't be a threat to scaly old me, right? She looked more afraid than I felt.

"Please forgive me." I watched her lower lip tremble, eyes still wide as she stepped slowly toward me with her hands behind her back. And I could almost imagine she approached a unicorn instead of a dragon man like me, but unicorns didn't exist. I gazed down into her soft eyes, imagining what her lips might taste like. Thinking that about a girl who seemed so pure made me want to slap myself. Her arm moved faster than I could track it. Everything went black.

"Ow!" My cheek rested on something smooth and cold. Yup, the floor. My vision was still a little blurry, but when I went to rub my eyes, I found my hands tied behind my back. Whatever had poked the tender spot on my head had another go. This time, I could only muster a groan.

"Tell me how to lift the wards, or I'll hit you again, dragon boy." The girl's voice wasn't menacing at all, but whatever she'd hit me with sure was.

"I can't. Ow!"

"You can, and you will."

"No, it doesn't work for me. Only Mother can open it now."

"Ugh. Not another mama's boy."

"What?" I moved my shoulder, tilting so I could look at my captor. Her hair was long and nut-brown with platinum streaks and tips. I'd seen her before, after Nox's trial. "Didn't you help save my Alpha? Why are you robbing me?"

"I'm not robbing you." She flipped her hair back over her shoulder. "I'm just taking something that belongs to my people."

I glanced at the small heap of trinkets on the floor next to her. Narrowing my eyes and calling on my dragon, I scrutinized them for magic energy. Sure enough, they swirled with golden Luck energy I couldn't decipher. This girl could only be Yoshi Ichiro's daughter.

"Look, I get that Tanuki are the best with Luck magic. Really, I do." I shook my head once and had to stop. It hurt too much. "But you don't understand dragon shifters. Once something's in the hoard, you can't claim reparations or eminent domain or whatever lawyerese your dad sent you over here to recite. My mom's like Bruce Banner and Doctor Jekyll recombined themselves a lovechild way back in the dark ages. You won't like her when she's angry. Even I don't, and she sort of raised me."

"Your mother sort of raised you?" One perfectly curved eyebrow lifted. "That's a weird thing to say."

"I give you a warning about an irate dragon lady, and her parenting skills are what you focus on?" This girl was driving me crazy. Also, my hands were falling asleep. I focused on scaling them over with a partial shift. Maybe that'd make it easier to get out of whatever she'd used to tie them together. But my dragon didn't want to escape. Under other circumstances, I wouldn't want to either.

"I can't heed your warning, so I figured I'd take the fun in dysfunctional for five hundred, Alex." She shrugged, making the buttons on the front of her blouse strain a little. I looked away.

"You're an odd one." That was the understatement of the decade. This girl was battier than a bat shifter. She'd broken into a dragon hoard, for Tiamat's sake!

"Back at you, Trogdor." She smiled, batting her eyes.

"Hey, only my friends are allowed to insult me like that. And none of my friends would ruin my life by trying to break in here." That made me stop and think, a tough task while recovering from the knock on my noggin. How had she broken in, anyway?

"And if your friends jumped off the Pell Bridge, I wouldn't." She flipped her hair over one shoulder, batting her eyelashes. I paid attention in an entirely inappropriate way. She looked younger than Lynn Frampton, but a Tanuki could physically be nineteen and chronologically be fifty with a Luck charm. And there was a whole pile of them, right in front of her.

"Maybe you'd be better off jumping from a bridge. Mother doesn't pull her punches, but I'm her only child. I could put in a good word if you try being a little nicer to me." I hadn't just said something that smarmy? Oh, yeah, I had. I'd meant it that way, too.

"How about you keep these a secret from your mom?" She

held up a pair of Luck-infused cufflinks, then tucked them down the front of her shirt. "That'd give me tons of motivation to be—" She leaned over, her face close to mine. "Nice."

"Hey!" I wriggled, trying to stop her from sitting on my lap. It was no use. My dragon had woken up and given her his full attention. He liked what he saw even more than I did. That only made things worse. I rolled my eyes. "Why do you need my help? Can't you just get out the way you came in?"

"No such luck with the wards up." She shrugged, then gazed into my eyes. Most girls flinched when they were dragonish, but not her. "That's a striking shade of red, Blaine. You're very attractive. Why didn't anyone bother telling me that, I wonder?" She put one arm around my neck.

"Gah!" I pushed with my feet, forcing my weight against the wall I leaned on so I could stand. She fell off my lap with a shrill little shriek. Mother would be back soon, and I couldn't let her see me with the burglar on my lap. And there was something else, too. "Stop trying to distract me. You got in here. You get yourself out. It's not like there's a shortage of Luck charms in here."

I flexed my arms, hearing the purr of tearing fabric as my hands pulled free of whatever she'd tied me with. Smoke trailed from my nose, hazing my vision. I always hated that. I focused and turned it into a ring instead so I could see what in Tiamat's name I was doing. Then, I lowered my shoulder and rushed her.

She stepped out of the way at the last possible second. That was a good thing since I had to swerve to avoid smashing a vase worth over a million dollars. I turned to face her again, reaching out to grapple her this time. I got her blouse. Instead of trying to get away, she threw herself at me.

We went down together, rolling around the marble floor in a tussle, unlike any fair fight I'd had. She grabbed handfuls of my hair, pulling my head every which way. I tried to get a grip without seeming like I was copping a feel. The way she writhed in my grasp made that almost impossible.

I felt the air change before I realized the door had opened. I'd been crawling, trying to get off the floor from my hands and knees with the Ichiro girl clinging around my neck and waist with her arms and legs. Her skirt had flipped up, giving Mother and my stepdad a show she might have fully intended. She laughed, obliterating any vestige of innocent girlishness left in my opinion of her.

"Blaine Carter Harcourt, put that girl down this instant." Mother's voice was quiet, which rated Defcon 1 on the Hertha Harcourt warning system. I'd rather hear her shout than whisper any day of the week.

It took effort, but I got on my knees and held my hands up like I was in the weirdest jazz dance routine ever. The girl hung on, clinging even tighter. There were women I'd had one night stands with who hadn't held me that close.

"Miss Ichiro, I believe?" Super stepdad, Wilfred Harcourt, to the rescue. He walked around alongside us, staring down. Then, he did something wildly inappropriate. He stuck his hand down the front of the Ichiro girl's shirt. He plucked something from her cleavage, then held it up. The cuff-links gleamed from between his thumb and first finger.

I stared at Mother, my eyes so wide I felt they might pop out of their sockets and roll around on the floor. She smiled. Not at her weak fart of a socially appropriate husband. Not at her bewildered son. She stood there grinning at the Ichiro girl. I blinked, probably saving my poor eyeballs from a bug's squashed fate.

"Well, Wilfred, it seems Blaine's got something to do besides mope around the manor during his Spring Break."

"I beg your pardon?" Mother never called him Wilfred unless she had something devious spinning the hamster wheel I suspected of running her brain. She was about to drop some serious trouble in my lap on top of the Tanuki who wouldn't leave.

"Yes. My son is just the young man to handle this particular problem." Her smile brightened in wattage until it could have made the moon and stars give up and go home.

"What?" I didn't realize my jaw had dropped until the Tanuki chick's thumb pushed it closed. I ground my teeth and pushed her me before speaking again. "Handle this problem?" I pointed at the girl. "She broke into your hoard. Yours, not mine."

"True, but it's a pile of wealth you'll be in charge of someday." Her lips closed over her teeth, but the corners of her mouth tilted so much they could have been tied to her ears. "And I hear you've got quite the reputation for taking care of little mysteries like this when they crop up for your friends. The least you can do is help your beloved mother with this one small matter."

"Oookay?" I stood up, brushing myself off. Movement snagged the corner of my eye. I turned, my elbow swinging ahead of me. I knocked a delicately rounded shoulder. Trinkets clattered to the floor. The girl put both hands to her cheeks, her mouth making a little round "o" of whatever emotion thieves have when they get caught. I grabbed her arm, knowing I'd better keep a hand on her if she weren't in my direct field of vision.

"I understand the reason behind your choice, wife, but shouldn't we at least tell him—" My stepdad shut his mouth mid-sentence when Mother snapped her fingers.

"You know nothing. This is my hoard, the one that brought your title to this marriage." Mother snaked her arm through her husband's. "I'll borrow some of Miss Thurston's faculty and set up wards around the property instead of just the vaults. That way, she can only run far enough to provide some amusement."

My stepdad straightened, throwing his shoulders back. He let her escort him to the doorway, then paused. His sibilant whispers carried a hint of pleas. I couldn't look away because I knew Wilfred had provoked her instead of swaying her.

"I won't tell him or her. And I think Mr. Waban can also help with those wards, come to think of it." The sound of Mother's heels clicking away against the marble punctuated the finality of that last statement. I felt bad for Wilfred, whose shoulders sagged like half the hoard's contents rested on them. I didn't much like Taki Waban either, and I suspected the feeling was more than mutual. Make one horse joke at the wrong time, make an enemy of the new ice dragon librarian.

I turned, reaching out to grasp the girl's other arm. Her head bowed so low I could only see the top of it. She didn't make a sound. I rolled my eyes. This had to be more manipulation, an attempt to get me to let her go. I headed down past the display case I'd caught her climbing and across an aisle to another curio cabinet, much less ornate than the other one. Then, I let go of one of her arms, pulled open the glass-fronted door, and took out a pair of bracelets. I slapped one on her wrist and the other on mine. The magic activating felt like a static shock to the face. I sneezed. She didn't, but looked up.

"What did you do?" She reached for the bracelet, trying to unfasten the clasp. I chuckled.

"These are Faerie Tithing bracelets. You can't go further than an acre from me without passing out." I let go of her.

"Doesn't that mean you also pass out?" Her smile was gentler than Mother's, but no less charged with mischief.

"No." I lied. I hate lying about my knowledge.

"Oh, you." Her laugh cascaded like that string orchestral stuff my stepdad listened to. "You're not the only artifact expert in the world, you know."

"Think what you want." I turned, heading for the door. "That acre includes height, you know. I'm going to the third floor, and this is the basement. It's a building constructed for dragons the size of football fields. You do the math."

"Don't you want to know my name?" Soft footsteps hurried to catch up with me. I glanced down, relieved to see she wore moccasins instead of stilettos like Mother.

"I don't care." But that was another lie. I did. But I didn't want to give her the satisfaction of asking her for it.

CHAPTER TWO

Kimiko

We walked in silence through the dragon-sized halls and up two flights of stairs. This wasn't at all how I had imagined the evening going. I should have been in and out of there once I had my mitts on the luck charms I'd come for. I didn't understand why, either. The charm I'd burnt when Blaine came in should have let me slip out before the wards engaged. Instead, I got confronted by three dragon shifters for the price of one. And Blaine was nothing like what I'd expected. Either Beth had misrepresented him, or he was a giant scaly liar. After his attempt to fool me about the Tithing Bracelets, my money was on liar.

When he ushered me into a room almost as big as the entire first floor of my dad's house, I thought maybe my Luck would change. I put on my most vulnerable face, slouching a little to make my blouse look more disheveled. I wish I could say he didn't bother looking at me. He glared. I'd royally pissed him off. I shouldn't care, and told myself I didn't as the door closed behind him with a hollow thud. But I was a giant furry liar. A pair of liars, then, but nothing at all like a matched set.

There were four sets of double doors, with mirrors lining the walls between them. It felt like being in a glass house. I wondered who or what this room had been designed for, then shrugged. It didn't matter. I was used to being trapped in a place I didn't want to be, although not when so much was at stake beyond my boredom.

I decided to check out the amenities. One set of doors led to the most luxurious bathroom I'd ever seen. The shelves held plush towels, the cabinets all the lotions and potions a girl could want. I ran a bath, knowing the time it'd take to fill that huge Roman-style tub gave me a chance to check out the rest of the room.

A walk-in closet the size of a regular person's bedroom held neat rows of clothing for every occasion. All of it was feminine, not all of it in the colors I favored, but enough to make me wonder what in the name of Lady Luck could be going on here. Everything was my size, even the shoes. I leaned over, sniffing a dress. It smelled new with still a trace of the plastic it must have been wrapped in during shipping. I ran to a dresser, relieved to find only stretchy bras and underwear. No one had measured me in my sleep or snooped through my closets to suss out what size I wore. Whoever had estimated my dress size had to have a tailor's eye, though. Or an appraiser's. Someone was creepy in the estate of Harcourt, and my gut told me it wasn't Blaine.

I went to one nightstand. It had a locking drawer, with the key still in it. Someone wanted to give me the illusion of privacy, then. The glass on the walls made me wonder, though. Before stowing anything, I went to one mirror and pressed a finger to the surface. I knew the test wasn't the be-all and end-all, but it'd work as step one. The mirrors were set into the walls, stretching half the height to the cavernous ceilings the entire Harcourt mansion had. Even though there was a visible gap between my finger and its reflection, it could still be transparent.

With my hands cupped, I leaned against the glass. Trying to peer into any room that might be behind it would give anyone watching a rude surprise, but I couldn't see anything. Knocking made a thud near my ear, but a hollow reverberation higher up. I had a theory. I rapped on every single mirror to test them.

Half of them made the hollow sound. I marked each one with a touch of magic in the lower corner. There wasn't anyone watching right behind the mirrors, but there were probably concealed cameras high up. It's what I'd do if I were head of a family of paranoid dragons. One thing I didn't bother with was looking for bugs. I already knew I didn't talk in my sleep from my time in The Academy dorms, and I could wait to try to communicate with my ally until a bit later.

If I stood just right at the locking nightstand, I could conceal what I did with my purse before locking it up. I twisted and hunched, then peeked into my handbag to make sure my secret weapon was still in there. Once locked, I brought the key to a jewelry box on one dresser. A simple gold chain worked to string it on around my neck. Someone else in the house might have a copy of the key, but this was the best I could do for now. I'd have to rely on my Luck to keep anyone from looking in the drawer and the bag. I went back and touched the drawer again, with Luck magic, this time, hoping it'd be enough.

Back in the bathroom, I tossed a raspberry bath bomb into the water and threw my clothes at a hamper, not caring when they missed. With my hair pinned against my head by a studded gold clip, I sank into the hot water I hoped would ease my body and mind. When I opened my eyes, a slender glass of something that smelled suspiciously like plum wine sat on the tile edging the tub. Someone knew I was over twenty-one, then.

I didn't dare emerge from the bubble-covered water, so I tried checking the bathroom for magic. I should have done that to begin with, in the bedroom, too. Some Tanuki I was, forgetting an important thing like that. I blamed Blaine Harcourt with his jerky attitude and dreamboat eyes instead of myself.

After a few moments, I realized that a decorative gilt bamboo stand in one corner was actually a hiding place for a Brownie. I'd known Hertha Harcourt and the Sidhe Queen were tight, but not enough to assume it merited pure Faerie servants painting themselves to match the decor. I chalked it up to dragon craziness and decided to be friendly for the moment.

"Um, hi." I nodded to the stick-like creature in the corner. "How did you know I like plum wine?"

"The same way I knew your dress size." The brownie swayed a little, creaking slightly. "Your hostess mentioned it."

"Huh. That's weird." I sighed, relaxing back into the bath. I didn't have to worry about a Brownie ogling me since they had no gender, like the other pure Faeries. But I shouldn't ask them any more questions. If they served the Harcourt family, I'd just be digging my own grave and owe them by accident. "Well, thanks again." I picked up the glass, raised it, and sipped.

"I—" The Brownie creaked and crackled, twisting in a nonexistent breeze. "You're most welcome, Miss Ichiro."

"None of that 'Miss' stuff. Call me Kim." I winked. "Anyone who brings me wine this good deserves to be on a first-name basis."

"I understand." They straightened, a sign that they were at ease. "You consider it advantageous to be friendly with the help."

"You have some experience with Tanuki guests, then." I sipped the excellent wine again, letting the fruity and lightly fuzzy taste roll over my tongue a few times. I breathed in to enjoy its bouquet as well. "And anyone serving the Harcourts who gilds themselves goes above and beyond. Kudos! You must be one of the most highly-valued servants here."

"There's a mortal saying about making assumptions."

"Yeah, yeah." I waved my free hand in a dismissive gesture. "I'm an optimist."

"Tread carefully, Kim." Their voice sighed like a breeze through branches. "Your hostess has been waiting for something like this to happen for decades."

I swallowed more wine because there was no other way to get around the lump forming in my throat. When the bathwater cooled, I got out and dried off. A robe on the inside of the bathroom door covered me until I could slip into a silky nightgown from the dresser.

I took a deep breath, closing my eyes to tighten my focus. When I opened my eyes, I scanned the room for magical listening devices. Then, I checked under furniture and in decorations for the kind garden-variety humans used. It seemed whoever installed the cameras hadn't worried about listening in. The bed was comfortable and warm, the room quiet and almost peaceful once I turned the lights off.

"Ismail?" I knew my ally could hear me, but he didn't answer. Why would he? The creature I'd roped into helping me was under one of the oldest kinds of Faerie contracts. I still had him on the hook for one more go, and I bet comforting a despairing Tanuki wasn't on his list of favorite pastimes. I rolled over, turning my back on the nightstand, and shut my eyes.

The Brownie's ominous words kept me awake for a while. I'd almost stolen the thing I broke into the hoard to get, but if Hertha Harcourt had plans for me, I might not get one of her Luck charms where it needed to be in time. I flushed with anger and shame, turning my head so my tears fell on the sateen pillowcase instead of all over my face. The Harcourts had plenty of Luck charms in just that one vault. And dragon shifters got to be immortal all on their own, but Tanuki needed those charms to survive. If we used too much Luck without a charm, we aged faster. If we used up the last charm, years we'd borrowed ran out like sands through an hourglass.

I'd had no idea Dad's lapel pin was his last Luck charm when I nicked it. And then, Josh Dennison lay dying in front of the Temple to Music. With my brother engaged to his sister, the wolf shifter was practically family. If I hadn't burned the Luck in Dad's pin, then Josh would be in the ground, dead from a cockatrice scratch.

The only thing I'd ever been good at was sneakiness. That meant Dad's best chance was me doing a little stealing. I'd broken into the hoard to save my father, even though he'd never ask me to. If he didn't live to give me away at my wedding or hold his grandchildren, it'd be my fault. I couldn't live with the guilt, and I'd thought for one brief shining moment that I wouldn't have to. But Blaine Harcourt had ruined my entire plan by walking in before I was done and then not telling me how to get out in time. And Hertha Harcourt never gave things away. Trying to negotiate with her would come at a steep price.

As I drifted off, it occurred to me that I wasn't dealing with the dragon lady. She'd put Blaine in charge of me and my attempted theft. A week earlier, I'd have hoped he'd understand my predicament. But that was before I learned the up close and in person truth about him. Blaine Harcourt was every bit as paranoid and possessive as any other dragon shifter on the planet. He had to be the type of person to expect something precious from me in exchange for what he had in abundance. I was convinced he wouldn't help me, not even if I could get him somewhere private and tell him everything.

CHAPTER THREE

Blaine

I leaned on the door frame, thinking about knocking again. Just as I'd raised my hand, it opened. The girl glared, still wearing a shimmery nightgown. Her face was just as flawless-looking as it had been last night, although her eyes looked a little red around the rims. She'd been weeping, of course. I felt guilty, realizing she must have cried herself to sleep. But she'd broken in here, then clocked me one on the noggin. Why should I feel bad for her just because she was beautiful? That seemed like something my roommate Bobby would do, the Boy Scout. Had sharing a room with him made me soft, or just soft in the head?

I stuck my hand out, stopping the door as she tried to swing it shut. She rolled her eyes before I could do it myself. I stopped the trajectory of my eyeballs, not wanting her to think I'd copied her.

"What do you want?" Her scowl made her lips all pouty. I blinked, looking away from them. To think, I'd almost kissed her before she brained me. Stupid dragon hormones, always getting me in trouble.

"Uh, to ask if you want breakfast?" I tried smiling, but with the door crunching my fingers, it probably looked more like I had gas.

"No." Her stomach growled louder than a wolf shifter chasing a Gnome. She sighed. "Yes. I don't know. Shouldn't the Brownie just bring it, so I don't inconvenience you?"

"You've got a lot to learn about dragon hospitality." This time, I did roll my eyes. "And what Brownie?"

She stood there, chewing her lower lip, then she opened the door, inclining her head and waving with one hand to indicate I could come in. I stepped across the threshold but waited until she moved halfway across the room before shutting the door behind me and heading in. I didn't want her to brain me again.

Even though it'd take a high-ranking Faerie courtier to remove the bracelets, I was worried she might do something drastic like dislocating my thumb to try to take them off. I knew nothing about the Ichiro girl except that she had a habit of breaking out of secure boarding schools and into my mom's hoard. And that she drove me nuttier than a fruitcake.

"I'll be out in a minute. She grabbed her handbag from the nightstand, then something from the top drawer of the dresser and headed into the closet. The light went on when she shut the door, just like it did in all the closets at this mansion. I wondered exactly what kind of paranoia motivated Mother to make that addition.

I waited, listening to the clack of wooden hangers and rustle of fabric as she dressed. Instead of asking her about the Brownie again, I checked. This guest room was a mirror image of mine, so it was easy to find the likely places. Nothing. I headed for the bathroom even though that wasn't a great hiding place for water-phobic creatures like Brownies. Turning on the light nearly dazzled my eyes. The bedroom mirrors were shiny, but the shimmery decor in this bathroom was even more over the top. Nothing but towels, bath stuff, and that lame gilded pot of desiccated bamboo Mother insisted on having all over the house.

As I turned to go back into the bedroom, something creaked. Though the floors were covered with cushy mats, they were marble underneath. Besides, the sound came from the corner, not under my feet. Could the bamboo hide a Brownie? They looked like sticks, but it would have to be covered in gold paint to escape notice here.

"Ahem." The girl tugged my sleeve.

I turned in the doorway again, forgetting all about the Brownie. She'd just put on a simple sundress, but it made her look like a goddess. I wondered how a dress like that had ended up in her closet. It definitely wasn't one of Mother's last season items. Mother never wore pastels or floral prints.

"Um, okay." I turned my back on her, striding as fast as I could toward the door. "Breakfast. Follow me."

She did, a pair of gold ballet flats making muffled taps against the hall floors. She kept pace with me, something most of the girls back on campus had trouble with. I wondered how she managed, considering she couldn't be much more than five feet tall. I felt like the world's biggest idiot for not knowing her first name. Pride was one of my worst habits but swallowing it hadn't been something I was willing to do without the threat of an emergency or a bigger dragon. So why did I want to gulp down the whole lump for this thieving Tanuki?

"Look, I'm sorry about last night." I didn't even glance at her. I was so nervous. "How I said I didn't care what your name was and all that. I'm a class-A jerk even according to my friends, but Mother's crazy-intimidating. We're stuck together for at least the rest of the week, so, let's call a truce. How about it?"

"A truce has terms, Harcourt." I glanced sideways at a sudden movement only to find her braiding a strand of that glossy tawny-tipped hair of hers. Braiding and walking at the same time? Dexterity hadn't been her dump stat.

"Okay. So, what will it take to get your agreement?"

"I know you won't take these bracelets off and let me go. How about something fun? This is a billionaire's mansion. There's got to be loads of things to do in here, and I need something to take my mind off my problems."

"I think maybe you should be thinking about your problems, though." Where in Tiamat's name was all this eggshell-walking coming from? She was a girl with Luck magic who turned into a little furry creature. I was the son of a billionaire who turned into a fire-breathing dragon. And she'd broken in here. I should be all Rhett Butler, not giving a damn. But how could I deliver zingers and sick burns if I didn't even know her name? And why didn't I want to?

"You just assume I'm not thinking about them all the time already?" She sniffed.

I turned my head to look at her, noticing the liquid sheen in her eyes complete with moisture at the corners. It felt like someone had just dropped an anvil in my belly. She kept on walking alongside me, her eyes on the marble her feet had yet to cross. The section of lower lip that wasn't in her teeth trembled lightly. I couldn't look away, not from someone so beautiful and so miserable at the same time. Big stupid mistake.

I fell on my tail, a side-effect of walking right into one of the pedestal tables Mother insisted on putting at every hallway inter-section. The glass urn full of red apples tilted toward me, so I flung my arms up to shield my face from the inevitable rain of ruined fruit and glass shards. Maximum dexterity Tanuki girl caught it, righted it, then took an apple to polish on her sleeve. If I hadn't been a shifter, I wouldn't have been able to track her movements. I'd have thought the urn hadn't fallen, and she just picked up an apple while I wasn't watching.

I looked up, blinking. She stretched a hand down to me, the

mist of tears gone from her eyes and a small smirk playing at the corners of her mouth. Something was off about her. I'd seen a mask slip but wasn't sure which emotion was genuine, the sadness or the mockery.

I put my hand in hers, letting her try to pull me to my feet on her own. She tugged and strained, huffing out an upward breath that blew her bangs off her forehead. A small star-shaped scar hid under there, gone from view before I could be sure it was more than a trick of the light or my imagination. The mark was tantalizingly familiar, and my first impulse was to brush aside her hair to get a better look. I didn't. Instead, I got my feet under me and finally stood up. When she let go of my hand, I felt a warm tingle where it had been.

"Thanks." I tucked a lock of hair behind my ear. "Look, this is going to go better if—"

"Kimiko." She scrutinized the shiny red fruit. "You know these are poisonous, right?"

"Yeah, like my mother." I shrugged. "Well, technically, she's venomous, and her breath is poisonous."

"Oh?" She placed the apple gently atop the others in the glass urn. "Really? How did you end up—"

"My bio-dad was a Fire dragon." I beckoned, then headed around the stupid table and its container of quietly deadly apples. "Mr. Harcourt isn't this baby's daddy. This kid is not his son."

"Weird." She glanced at me, then paid more attention to where she was going. Good on her. "I thought she married him back in the 80s."

"She did. I took decades to hatch."

"Wait." She held the hand she'd helped me up with in front of her, palm facing in. "You don't feel like a reptile."

"Neither do platypi."

"Platypuses."

"Whatever." I rolled my eyes. I usually only tolerated grammar corrections from Lynn for Bobby's sake. "Anyway, we're more like those than reptiles."

"If you were a character in a novel, you'd be the chosen one." Kimiko chuckled. It was low and throaty, not squeaky like I'd imagined.

"Good thing I'm not, then." I turned left down a narrower hallway. The aroma of cinnamon waffles wafted along toward us.

The kitchen was spacious and spotless, as usual. Kimiko stopped by the door, looking around at all the empty space. I had no idea what kind of kitchen she was used to, but this clearly wasn't it. Hoping she'd follow, I moseyed over to the counter where Gomer stood finishing spiced pears to go with the waffles. I leaned on the marble at enough of a distance to let him work and waited.

"Morning, Gomer."

"Good morning, young Master Harcourt."

"Oh, come on, Gomer. You don't need to get all Alfred Pennyworth on me. Kimiko's not exactly a formal guest and Mother's out for the rest of the morning."

"Well, then. Morning yourself, Blaine the Pain." The old Goblin cackled. "You want a waffle, make it yourself." He opened the iron, then flipped his waffle on a plate, which he took with him to one of the six stools at the breakfast bar.

I splooshed batter on the hot cast iron, not quite filling it, then closed it, not caring. It was food. I cared about what it tasted like, not how it looked. I dragged it onto my plate when it was done. Flipping was the territory of master chefs like Gomer. Mother had given him a job back in the 60s when tithing to the Sidhe Queen instead of the Goblin King had gotten him disowned and kicked out of the house by his family. They shouldn't have been surprised. The Seelies liked their rules, and any good chef has to follow recipes or suffer the consequences.

When I turned to top my waffle with spiced pears and fresh whipped cream, I almost knocked into Kimiko. She was licking.

The. Serving. Spoon. For the whipped cream. I had no idea how long she'd been at that, but it sent me headlong toward a feverish fit. I reached out, snatching the spoon away and holding it over my head where she couldn't reach. As if that'd do any good at that point.

"How's anyone else supposed to enjoy this whipped cream now?"

"What's your problem, anyway?" She crossed her arms over her chest, then raised an eyebrow. "Afraid of girl cooties, Young Master Harcourt?" She actually made air quotes around the title.

I mumbled something about no one deserving this kind of thing, then tossed that spoon in the sink and got another. Relief washed over me as I saw her flipping the waffle iron closed instead of licking the bowl. She was a Tanuki, not a cat shifter. That was who I'd expect to violate a bowl of whipped cream. I daubed some on top of the pears I'd already taken, then sat a few seats down from Gomer. He'd given me grief about sitting too close before, something about hidden cameras. Goblins were almost as paranoid as dragon shifters.

Kimiko sat down with a plate more cream than waffle. She dug in, taking my statement about her not being a formal guest seriously. She was done before I reached the halfway mark. Leaning on her elbow overlooking the empty plate, she grinned.

"So, what do you have planned for us?"

"Fun, as promised, Kimiko."

"I was having fun before with the bowl of whipped cream." She smirked. "Well, at least the most fun you could have alone with that sort of thing."

"Trust me, what I have planned is all fun all the time." I couldn't help but smirk back at her.

Gomer's throat cleared a warning, reminding me it shouldn't be fun. I was supposed to be Kimiko's warden, not her friend. I wasn't sure whether she'd let me be either.

CHAPTER FOUR

Kimiko

The game room was fantastic. I could almost forgive Blaine for being such a spoilsport about the whipped cream. It had a dartboard, billiards table, ping-pong, air hockey, even an arcade-style DDR console. But the best part was the setup on the west wall. A screen stretched from one corner to the other, towering over my head. It had just about every kind of console that had existed since Atari plus a gaming rig attached to it. I had to sit down for a moment and just stare.

"This fun enough for you?" Blaine turned to face me, leaning against a decorative pillar. His smirk curled his lips in a way I wished I didn't find so interesting. I hadn't been lying back in the hoard; he *was* the most attractive man I'd ever laid eyes on. But he was keeping me here against my will with a magical device, preventing me from saving my father's life. I had to take a deep breath before all my frustration rose to color my cheeks and gave my anger away. So, I closed my eyes and thought about the video games.

"I don't even know where to start." I stood up, tracing one finger along the satiny-smooth wood trim of the billiard table. I felt him watching me again, and this time, the heat that threatened to color my cheeks wasn't from anger. That sucked. I headed to the dartboard, turned my back to Blaine, and picked up one projectile.

"I'd prefer you choose our activity, but if you're that overwhelmed, I can think of—"

He ducked in time, but barely. The dart had pinned a strand of his hair to the wall when it hit. "Um, okay. Darts it is." He pulled the projectile out of the wall, his sauntering pace casual as he headed toward me.

How dare he saunter after an attack like that? How dare he dodge that fast? After being klutzy in the hall earlier, he should have been an easy target. Then again, he was a dragon. Maybe I shouldn't have underestimated him.

I clenched my fists at my side as he took my attack in stride like some kind of lame joke. It wasn't. He didn't know I'd stuck the tip of the dart into the sliver of poison apple up my sleeve. I had to either incapacitate him so he wouldn't see how I got us out of the mansion, or convince him to help me. I didn't think much of my chances with the latter.

I beat him handily at darts, scoring seven more points than he did. It was easy. All I had to do was imagine his mother's face on the bullseye. I got tired of it pretty quickly, though. I headed over to the games, reaching out for a controller shaped like a guitar. Behind me, I heard him pick something up, and the screen lit. He took one of the other guitar controllers and got the game on. He'd played through it, and everything was unlocked, of course. I went straight to the hardest song, chuckling with irony at the juxtaposition of the band name and my opponent.

"Um, Kimiko, maybe…"

I selected Expert and started the game. What followed can't be described. Well, I guess I can say that trying to describe it reminds me of that song *Tribute* by Tenacious D. You know the one? They tell a story about how they beat a shiny demon's challenge to play the greatest and best song in the world. They do it but forget the entire winning song afterward. The song they tell the story with is pretty epic, but they say it can't match that one glorious lonely-road concert. Playing expert-level *Through The Fire and Flames* with Blaine Harcourt was like that, even though it didn't sound anything like that song.

I used to quadruple my allowance game-sharking the kind of boys who go on about fake gamer girls on that song. Blaine might have done the same. Might. It was getting harder to hate him or even just his guts. I still couldn't trust him, though. He'd never help me save my dad. I wasn't one of those Tinfoil Hatters he ran with over at PPC. I couldn't pretend he'd choose to help me over following his mother's orders. But he shook my resolve even more when I set down my ersatz guitar.

Blaine threw back his head and laughed. His own controller hung from the strap around his neck, forcing me to imagine him as a big goofy kid playing pretend rock stars or something. Was this some other game, trying to make me like him? What was the point in that? I couldn't like him. He might want to act like my friend now, but once I got out of here with a Luck charm, he couldn't pretend to be anything else. Stealing from a dragon shifter's hoard would make me his enemy forever.

"You rock." He finally unslung the guitar and pointed at the screen. "That's the best score I've ever gotten, and it wouldn't have happened without you."

"Huh? But I beat you." I peered at the screen, realizing I'd been so caught up in my thoughts I hadn't bothered to look at anything besides my winning score. Blaine had beaten his old record by a respectable amount. "Well, you still lost. You big scaly loser." I stuck out my tongue.

"Hey, losing to you is better than sitting in here alone trying to outdo my old high score." He shrugged.

I had nothing to say to that. He'd grown up alone, then. It made more sense now, how he'd said his parents "sort of" raised him. I blinked, missing my brother, Ren, terribly all of a sudden. He'd be wondering where I was, maybe even thinking I'd taken off and left him alone to care for Dad as his aging drastically accelerated. I had to pull myself together. Before I could shake my head and snap myself out of it, a set of warmer than average hands were on my shoulders.

"Hey. I noticed you made a face like this earlier. You okay?" The unexpected warmth in his eyes had my knees wobblier than my first impression of the game room. I raised my hand halfway to the side of his face, twisting my wrist to rub my fingertips against the apple sliver up my sleeve. I could touch his lips, then move in and pretend I wanted to kiss him. He'd drop like a rock, and I'd be free to take him hostage to demand a Luck charm. I pulled away and headed for the door, blinking back tears.

"I'm just tired and thirsty. This building's sized for dragons the length of a football field. Come along, or let the tithing bracelets knock us out." I pushed the door open. "I don't care which happens."

I hurried down the hall, telling myself those weren't butterflies in my stomach as I hoped he'd follow. Then, I let the sliver of apple fall from my sleeve and wiped my fingers on my dress once he'd caught up with me. I couldn't poison him, especially since I wasn't sure how much apple would be enough to kill him in his human form. I tried to tell myself I was failing my father because Blaine behaved honorably and his mother was the real enemy, not because of those eyes and that smile.

I'd have to tell him Dad was dying, but not where Mrs. Harcourt had any chance of hearing. My father was running out of time, and I was the only one who could save him. I needed Blaine on my side.

CHAPTER FIVE

Blaine

I shouldn't have trusted a word Kimiko Ichiro said, but it was hard not to admire her skill at games. I hadn't been trounced so soundly since I played another dragon shifter in online mode. And I hadn't felt her use any magic, either, just her natural shifter abilities. That's why I was surprised to find her almost in tears after the win. I paced her down the hall, shortening my steps to go at her speed. She found the route leading to the kitchen on her first try, probably some kind of side-effect of studying the blueprints in preparation for the robbery or whatever. I shook my head. Why would such a talented girl like her do something so impossible and take such a risk? Why hadn't she just asked me?

I ignored the smell of slightly stale apple, catching a whiff of tea and the honey-seed cakes Mother always served to guests she wasn't just pretending to like. Before we reached the door, I held up a finger to signal a stop and quiet. Kimiko didn't argue or question me. Instead, I blinked as her ears furred over and rounded further out from her head. When she tucked her hair behind them, I saw they had pale, fluffy tufts at the centers, which matched the tips of the locks on her head. She leaned closer to the door. I joined her in eavesdropping. That particular pastime had helped me avoid trouble throughout most of my childhood. It made sense to me that a thief like her was used to listening in.

"Now, Hertha, there has to be some reason you've asked me here besides a thank-you tea." That was Headmistress Thurston talking, thank goodness. The tightness in my shoulders eased. It might have been the Sidhe Queen visiting, and I'd definitely been dropped from her nice list. Besides, the Headmistress was good people. She'd been the one to open PPC admissions to anyone with the grades, including dragons.

"Ulterior motives are like scales to dragons. You know my kind well, Henny." My mother actually sighed. "The break-in happened at a delicate time, as I'm sure you're aware. I can't tolerate having hoard security breached with something so precious inside, so I must know more about how it happened and why. I need Edgar Watkins."

I blinked. Professor Watkins had the hardest nose of any professor to stalk the halls of PPC in all its centuries, but his given name was Nate, not Edgar. I listened on, wondering whether the person Mother asked for might be a ghostly ancestor of his or something.

"I need Edgar Watkins too, with all the trouble we've been having on campus, but no one's seen him since poor Dahlia died and Henry got turned. Some people don't even seem to remember he exists."

"Are you sure about that?" I heard a clink as Mother put down her teacup. "Is Henry Baxter sure about that?"

"Perhaps you ought to send him an invitation for tomorrow evening."

"You know the reason I'm unable to do that." Mother sighed. "This is no time to invite a vampire inside my house."

"Understood. Still, an Air Magus like me isn't the right sort of person to ask about memories." I heard the Headmistress rattle an empty cup against her saucer. "Why not hire him? Send him an item to read if you can't have him here."

"I need Edgar in particular." I heard a series of four wooden taps that could only be Mother thrumming her fingernails on the table. "Some old business has come up as well."

"Then hire him to search for information about Edgar." I smelled cream and sugar, heard a crisp pour as the Headmistress refreshed her tea. "Although I'm not sure what the difference is between the two in your case."

"The difference is, the item in question can't leave the estate, he's directly linked to the old business I mentioned, and Unliving energy is too dangerous for the most vulnerable member of this household." What in Tiamat's name could Mother be talking about? I was the youngest and weakest Harcourt, and I hung out with Henry all the time.

Kimiko put her hands to her cheeks as calculation invaded her face like the Huns in China 200 years before the common era. Her ears flicked, pointing toward the door so she could listen in more closely.

"I've got no idea where Edgar Watkins is. Neither does his brother." The Headmistress sighed. "We're lucky he left us able to remember his name."

"Why not call your ex-husband, then? Whatever was his name again?" Mother's voice carried an emotion I wasn't used to hearing. Fear. This was one of the weirdest conversations I'd ever listened in on. Headmistress Thurston had lowered her voice to the point where I could only make out a few words of her answer.

"…Richard's been elusive just lately…"

"I understand it was a bad split, Henny, but you know what

they say. Keep your friends close and your enemies closer." I heard a rustle of fabric and faint creak as Mother sat back in her chair. "Hasn't he gotten around to Tithing, finally?"

My breath became like the vacuum of space in the silence that followed. I hadn't known the Headmistress's ex-husband was an untithed Changeling. According to rumor, the Headmistress and her husband had broken up over her open admissions policy. At his age, he had to be an extremely powerful Magus. No wonder the Queen kept on getting involved in College affairs. She'd want him to Tithe to her, not the King.

This was a development I had to tell the rest of Tinfoil Hat about as soon as possible, Spring Break or not. I reached for my phone, but Kimiko grabbed my arm. She pushed me against the wall next to the door, shaking her head to cover those Tanuki ears with her hair. I smelled Chanel Beige and realized Mother hadn't been sitting back. She'd been getting up.

I opened my mouth to tell Kimiko to get the heck out of dodge, but she had other ideas for camouflaging our eavesdropping. She pounced on me, toppling us both on to a small decorative fainting couch.

Well, that's a little inaccurate. I caught her. But I would have flung her away if Mother hadn't been about to walk through the door on my right. I wouldn't have let her get that close to me again unless it was another knock-down-drag-out like we'd had in the vault. So I closed my eyes, letting her put on whatever show she had planned. I felt her hair tickle my neck, her breath in my ear, and her hands in my back pockets. I stifled a sigh, fighting the urge to melt into her ministrations and let whatever happened happen. My dragon was all for that idea. Kimiko seemed to know what she was doing. It'd been a while for me, and she smelled like heaven. Well, except that hint of stale apple.

Apple? The only apples she'd been around that day were Mother's Evil Queen poison ones. I twisted my hands in her hair, anger at the fact she'd tried to slip me a mickey flip-flopping at the silken feel of her tresses against my skin. Like Forbidden Chocolate Ice Cream, Kimiko Ichiro was bad for me but felt so good at the same time. I needed help with the new information we'd overheard, but also some solid advice about how to outwit an alternately amorous and dangerous Tanuki.

"When you said you had another guest, I didn't think you meant this sort." Headmistress Thurston's arch tone could only go with an eyebrow position of the same name. I didn't dare look and find out, not even when Kimiko climbed off my lap to smile at the next two scariest ladies in my universe.

I couldn't look at Mother and wouldn't look at the Headmistress. That left me even more stuck with that Tanuki than the tithing bracelets made me. She'd managed to use our faux make-out session as cover for shifting her ears back to human shape. Her hair was still perfectly smooth though she rearranged her dress shamelessly. The flash of leg she showed made my throat dry. I thanked Tiamat that I was sitting down.

"It's good to see the two of you working things out." Mother sounded amused. For me, that was like hearing a funeral dirge. She'd think I'd charmed Kimiko and gotten some kind of information about how she'd broken in here. I had to get away long enough to give that another go.

"Yeah. We were looking for you, actually. I wanted to know if you'd let us through the wards later. You see, I'd like to take Kimiko out, show her around Newport a little." I didn't mention the bracelets, but Mother saw me twist mine around my wrist. I grinned down at my shoes. Mother would know I was fibbing if I looked her in the eye, but I always did the shoe stare when she caught me red-handed with a girl.

"We can arrange that." Mother's head tilted toward Kimiko instead of me.

I chanced a glance up and almost gasped. Headmistress Thurston looked like death. Her face was nearly as pale as a vampire's, and the circles under her eyes spoke of extreme exhaustion. She shouldn't have been so severely drained from putting up some wards with a few dragons and a handful of other Magi. She must have been casting like her Air magic was on an Everything Must Go Final Clearance Sale. But where and why? More stuff to talk over with Tinfoil Hat. I had to buy myself some time away from Mother and Kimiko though.

"How about we arrange it for dinner tonight, then?" I gazed at the back of Kimiko's head when Mother turned at the sound of my voice, trying to make my eyes look moonier than a were-wolf's. "Maybe seven o'clock?"

"That sounds perfect. I'll have the car take you to Freebody Park and make your reservations at The Spiced Bear for eight-thirty. That gives you time to walk and talk together." I wasn't sure because I wasn't exactly looking, but Mother might have winked. At Kimiko. No wonder the girl was so infuriating. My mother actually liked her. But why? Too many mysteries.

"I'll have to be heading back to campus now, Hertha." Head-mistress Thurston pulled her handbag up to her shoulder.

Mother made pleasantries with her guest as she escorted her down the hall and away. Before I could turn to look back toward Kimiko again, she squealed and flung her arms around me for the second time that day.

"Oh, Blaine!" She pulled back, gazing into my eyes. "You're not nearly as big a jerk as I thought you were. Thank you! You have no idea how awful it is being locked up everywhere I go by just about everyone I meet."

Instead of insulting her, I couldn't stop a smile from growing on my face. Her joy was infectious. Even if she wouldn't have made my top ten choices for company this week, it was better than sitting alone with my paranoia the whole time, just waiting for an Extramagus attack. I wondered whether she was wrong, whether maybe I did actually know about being locked up. It sure felt that way, but for me, it was more figurative than for her.

She went on about checking the weather and looking up the

restaurant, picking clothes, and getting ready. I let her until we parted at her door. Her hand on my cheek was almost like a peck and I almost damned the torpedoes and gave her an honest-to-goodness kiss. Almost, but that only counts in horseshoes. I locked the door to my room behind me and turned on the spyware interference devices I'd used everywhere since the Grim attacks on Campus during the inter-session.

It was time to phone a friend.

CHAPTER SIX

Kimiko

My stomach reminded me that we hadn't gotten snacks or a drink. Changing my ears to listen to the weird not-soccer-mom conversation had made me ravenous. I went into the bathroom, checking the decorative urn for my buddy the Brownie. They weren't there. In the bedroom, I found a panel on the wall next to the phone, with buttons by a list of names. One of them was that Goblin I'd met at breakfast, Gomer. Once my bag and the magical object hidden inside were locked in the nightstand, I pressed it.

"Gomer at your service." I chuckled, wishing I could risk replying with a cheerful "Bilbo Baggins at yours."

"Hi, Gomer." I wasn't sure whether his end of the console told him which room this was. "This is Kimiko Ichiro. I need some food. A snack, anything. If you don't mind, please." My stomach made a noise that reminded me of the time I lost one of my galoshes in the mud. Shifting made me wish I could go on the

Hobbiton diet, with Elevensies, Second Breakfasts, and all that jazz.

"Of course. I'll whip something up and have it sent along to the gold room." He chuckled. "Since you haven't stayed here before, make sure nothing's in the mandala on the rug. We don't much like ending up with laundry in the kitchen."

"Okay." I saw the design he was talking about. It must be some tangible marker for Vanishing or teleporting things. Faerie magic users being employed by a dragon family only made sense if you knew that dragons could see that kind of magic, unlike Magi. "Thanks, Gomer."

The intercom clicked off, and I felt more alone with my thoughts. I had to use this quasi-date to get Blaine on my side. So I'd need to plead my case about Dad while we walked, not in a place where friends or admirers of his mother might overhear. I didn't much care whether that happened before or after dinner. Still, I wished I had someone to talk to about this. The Brownie wasn't in the bathroom anymore. The only other option hadn't answered me last night, but maybe trying today was worth a shot. I took my purse out of the drawer and brought it into the bathroom, then turned on all the faucets.

"Hello, Ismail."

"Yes?" The deep voice was muffled, coming from my bag.

"Thank Lady Luck!" I set the purse on the counter and sat on the toilet lid so I could hear him better. "I thought you'd stopped speaking to me or something."

"No. I was sleeping, silly."

"Oh. I wasn't sure whether lamp-bound Djinn had a bedtime." I didn't admit how much more I didn't know about Djinn, which was pretty much everything besides the fact that they only granted each person three wishes while doing time in their family lamp. And that they were Faeries, so asking them too many questions meant you'd owe them.

"It's self-imposed. Let's just say I prefer to keep to the hours outside as much as possible. The last thing I want is lamp-lag if I ever stop serving in here." I heard something that could have been a sigh, but the lamp made me unsure of that. In any event, it was hard to try to read Ismail the Djinn the way I did other people. Trying to talk through metal was like listening through an old analog phone.

"Well, okay, then." I folded my hands in my lap and took a deep breath before continuing. "So, I have a date. With Blaine Harcourt."

"No Luck charms, but a date. Hmm. Did you let the dragon shifter catch you on purpose? I was wondering why you didn't wish yourself back home last night."

"He caught me, but not because I let it happen. He's something else. Anyway, the wards came down before I could wish. You already warned me that I'd have to wish before that. And then, Mr. Harcourt took away the charm I'd, um, pocketed."

"I see. You were right not to try after that. We Djinn are limited to Faerie powers, and even those can't Vanish people through wards."

"I'll have to find a way to get a charm and be outside wards so you can get me out of here, then. That's going to be hard with this thing." I twisted the tithing bracelet around my wrist three times.

"Yes. You'll need Blaine Harcourt with you unless you don't care about being in a coma." He sighed. "Or you'll need a highly ranked Courtier of the Goblin King to take it off of you ahead of time. That's an Unseelie bracelet set."

"That's not likely to happen in a house where the Queen's people are servants, Ismail."

"Ouch. Well, I'm sure you'll think of something."

"If only someone older and wiser had some advice." I didn't bother batting my eyes. While Djinn could read magical energy from inside their lamps, they couldn't actually see things like facial expressions unless they came out. Ismail was probably the most introverted Djinn I'd ever heard of. He hadn't even come out to grant either of my first two wishes. Most of them took any chance they could get to poof out.

"Yeah, if only." He chuckled before I could splutter.

"Relax, Kimiko Ichiro. Wear something that makes you feel pretty. Smile. You're a Tanuki and a good looking girl. Luck and circumstance are on your side even though coincidence might be iffy."

"Thanks, Ismail." I sat up. "You've gone so far above and beyond to help me ever since I, um, picked up your lamp." We both knew I hadn't just picked it up. I'd stolen it, of course, from a lab cabinet at The Academy.

"I'd tell you to fill out the customer satisfaction survey after I'm done helping you, but that's not one of the perks of my job." His last bit of advice faded out like someone turned down the volume. "Try to have fun."

I scratched my head, still not sure exactly how a Faerie bound in a lamp for who knows how long could joke about something like his enslaved state. Maybe he wasn't joking about being an introvert, or perhaps he'd taken a turn in the lamp to spare a family member that fate. Hopefully, I'd get a chance to ask him someday when all this was over. I couldn't risk any questions while I was master of the lamp though. Once the purse and Ismail's lamp were back in the nightstand, I got to work.

I had to make sure everything about me was perfect. I went into the closet to undress, putting the dress and everything under it in a hamper, then sticking the shoes back on the rack. After that, I shrugged into a robe and headed for the bathroom. In the shower, I washed my hair. And then I used the array of styling products and tools to make it as beautiful as possible. My stomach growled again when I smelled food. Gomer had come through.

Chewing watercress and cucumber sandwiches interspersed with sips of tea, I thought again about Ismail and his lamp.

Should I bring it out to dinner or leave it behind? If Blaine found it on me, he'd be suspicious for sure and maybe confiscate it. I couldn't afford to let him know I had a Djinn at my service until I also had a Luck charm and hopefully Blaine's cooperation or at least indifference. But how likely was I to win him over? Tapping my toe against the thick rug, I made a mental list of what I knew about him in particular versus dragon shifters in general.

Blaine was lonely. His joy at losing two different games in a row to me couldn't mean anything else. Dragon shifters supposedly liked their privacy. But everything I'd read on them had to do with the elders. I'd heard Blaine's mother call him a whelp which meant he was young. I knew nothing at all about young dragon shifters. Maybe the privacy preference had more to do with pre-Reveal society than dragon shifter instinct. Could dragons truly be misunderstood creatures, or was it just a tired old trope they used to get sympathy in this new age?

He also acted awkward around me even though Beth mentioned he was a huge flirt and a playboy. Physically, he seemed to be clumsier around me, too. He'd had trouble fighting me in the vault, fallen on his tail in the hall, and only just barely dodged my dart. Those things shouldn't have happened.

Of all the shifters on the planet, dragons were the most dangerous exactly because they had better enhancements than the other kinds. Why couldn't he handle a little Tanuki like me? Could it be Luck? Every Extrahuman and even a few humans had a trace of the magic I manipulated. I hadn't bothered checking Blaine's. Stupid of me. He might be low on Luck in general. But that was unlikely considering the number of Luck charms the Harcourts had stashed away here.

What if Blaine had Luck, but it had taken a turn for the worse? The implications of someone or something messing with a dragon's Luck were chilling. They had the best defenses of any shifter, both physically and magically. Only Tanuki could tamper with their Luck directly. Luck on its own just went where coincidence wanted it to. Only Magi could track coincidence, and barely any could nudge it. If Blaine hadn't been in direct contact with some other Tanuki, who wanted him dead instead of out of her hair, then he was at ground zero of a coincidence bomb greater and more terrible than Oz's reputation in that movie with the yellow brick road.

I put down the sandwich, appetite melted in the deluge of hunches like the Witch of the West in water. In the nearest mirror, I checked my own Luck. My throat went dry and my fingertips cold. Luck swirled around me as always, but in reverse. The usual light-gold glimmering swirls were laced with baleful red. My Luck had spun into one terrible twister. It wasn't in Kansas anymore.

I couldn't wait. I had to get eyes on Blaine right away and check his Luck. My hand curled tight and clammy around the cut-crystal doorknob. It didn't turn.

I was trapped. There had to be another way out of this room and over to the next. One set of double doors opened onto a tiny balcony. Blaine's room was to the right of that. The exterior wall had a decorative ledge. What could possibly go wrong?

CHAPTER SEVEN

Blaine

My anti-spyware devices stopped magical eavesdropping like Superman stopped trains, but I didn't want anyone overhearing mundanely. Usually, I'd blast some tunes, but that wasn't good for talking on the phone. So that's how I ended up sitting at my desk with an open laptop to see who could chat online. No Bobby, no Lynn. No Henry at lunchtime, of course. I put my head in my hands, abandoning all hope. The soft chime of an incoming message sounded, reminding me of GLaDOS. Maybe I should murder my useless computer before it threw me through a Portal or snuffed me. I sighed and stared at the screen instead. **Incoming message from Tony G**, it said.

Trogdor! Burninate any good books lately? Apparently, cat shifter families didn't bother going on out-of-town Spring Break vacations.

Va fa Napoli, Tony. My Italian might be rusty, but I used plenty of the most popular local swear words in the living languages I spoke.

Woah, dude. No need to bust out the potty mouth. Chill. Oh, wait, you can't. :p

Shut up and leave me alone. Tony Gitano was the last person I wanted to ask about this stuff.

No. I have news. Did you hear Ren's sister Kimiko's missing? Gossip and bird-watching were Tony's favorite pastimes.

She's not. If we'd been talking in person, he'd have gotten the hint that I didn't want to say more. Probably wouldn't have mattered. He didn't care about hints or me not wanting to talk to him most of the time.

Um, no. She is. Ren's freaking out. Just saw him two minutes ago. Why hadn't I thought of her older brother before now? The last thing we needed was a pissed off Selkie swimming over and scaling the cliffs outside.

Get offline and catch him, tell him she's fine.

OMG WTF. You. Did. Not. Not with your packmate's sister? Assumptions like that are why talking to a shady excuse for a LOLCat rankled so much.

He's your packmate, too, cat-man.

Yeah, but she ain't at my house while her brother's on the warpath. Josh'll have kittens.

Let him. I don't care what Beowulf thinks.

Wow, you really like this girl.

No. I don't. She's a giant pain in my ass. And nothing happened. She's just staying here.

Whatever. So, why are you online if you have a guest nothing happened with yet? Something hinky going down?

None of your business. It absolutely was not. But that sort of thing hadn't stopped Tony from butting in before.

Well, no one else is around. Henry and Maddie left for Vermont last night. Everyone's gone but me. They all went home.

Josh, isn't in Providence?

Negatory. He took Nox to Cape Cod.

Fewmets. Of course, Josh could go out of town. No Extramagus hunting him down anymore. But he knew I was next, and he just left? After I bailed his mate out of losing her magic and everything? *I'm stuck with the guy who flips out over laser pointers.*

I'll overlook the extra helping of verbal abuse. So what gives? Maybe I can help.

You can't. I really thought he couldn't. I needed another brain on this mess, and Tony's was always on how to trick friends and be a bad influence on people.

You can spend all your time arguing or give me the 411 and let me try. I put my head in my hands before making a decision and putting my fingers back to the keys.

Fine. Mother wants to hire some Psychic named Edgar Watkins, The Headmistress's ex is a Changeling. Also, Kimiko's here because I caught her in Mother's hoard trying to steal Luck charms.

Wait, Rick Thurston's a Changeling? Thought he was a Magus. But I hadn't mentioned the ex's name to Tony. Hadn't remembered it until he mentioned it. How had he known? Hinky cat-bastard.

He's both. Apparently, that happens sometimes.

What kind?

I closed my eyes. I should know, but I just couldn't remember. I had to have either read it somewhere or overheard it, right? Why was the Headmistress's ex-husband slipping my mind like a greased pig? The messaging program chimed again.

You don't remember either, huh, Trogdor?

No. Feels like it's on the tip of my brain, though.

Same. Anything else?

You really are useless.

Hey, I was going to take what you gave me and go look Ricky up in the Extrahuman Registries.

Oh. Sorry. Well, do it quick. The Headmistress could be an extra on The Walking Dead. Not like Henry, the fictitious zombie kind. Something's got her magically exhausted to the point where she could end up in the hospital.

Madonn.

Hey, you make me quit the cuss words, and then you go and do it?

Go to Naples, Blaine. Look, I'm sending you an Extrahuman Registry link from Olivia's PLEXIS Nexus ID. I did not want to know how he'd gotten that. And then I gotta go. Goombas on the move.

Um, what are you doing, playing Super Mario?

No. It's way more important than that. Look, I'm out of contact for a bit. Keep messenger open on your phone if you go anywhere.

No. Go jump in a lake, Tony.

Seriously, promise you'll keep messenger open.

All right, fine. At that point, I was just glad Tony didn't make me promise to answer it.

I shut down Messenger on the laptop and logged in on my phone. Then, I stood up to pace the room. And that's when I saw Kimiko Ichiro dangling from the railing outside my window like the last autumn leaf in a breeze. I dropped the phone and bolted for the balcony doors, flinging them inward to open them. I caught her by the wrist just in time, but her hand was so clammy she almost slipped my grip, anyway. Her eyes were wide and glassy, and when I hauled her up over the rail, she trembled like a fracking earthquake. I put her on my bed before I realized she was wearing nothing but a shiny satin bathrobe.

Anger kicked up the furnace in my gut like someone had poured butane on it. Smoke hazed my vision, probably hers too since I grabbed her by the shoulders and leaned in until our noses almost touched. Kimiko's lips were slightly parted, her head tilted back, but the whites of her eyes and the pinpoint pupils meant she was afraid instead of amorous. Good on her. At least she was the kind of girl who respected the fact an angry dragon had her in his clutches. But her gaze was unfocused.

"What in the name of the First Egg were you doing out there?" I clamped down harder on her shoulders. "I let the poison apple attempts slide, but this. Is. Madness."

"Blaine, it's your Luck." She shook her head, eyes still wider than the stratosphere. "Your Luck's corrupted, gone bad."

"Oh. Sorry." I let go of Kimiko's arms, hoping I hadn't hurt her. "Huh. I can't think of anyone who'd want me to be unlucky." I blew more smoke from my nose, unable to find the focus needed to make rings. "Can you?"

"No. But whoever it is messed with mine, too."

My phone blasted *Werewolves of London* by Warren Zevon. Josh was calling. I took a deep breath, then released Kimiko's shoulders.

"I need to answer that." I stabbed a finger at the air between us then waggled my eyebrows. "Don't move from that bed or you're crispy critters." She blinked and put her hand over her mouth, shoulders shaking around a suppressed giggle.

"What's up, wolf?" I held the phone to my ear.

"Put me on speaker." Josh sounded more like his dad than himself. Something had him in adult mode, not the kind of "adulting" you did alone on Cape Cod with your mate, either.

"What?"

"You heard me. Your companion needs to listen to this, too."

"I don't have a—"

"Bullshit. Speaker or you don't get the information I have." The absolute worry in his voice damped down my fire like a wet blanket. I pressed the button. "The Sprite told me you were next the night I fought the cockatrice, Blaine. They just interrupted Nox and me in the middle of lunch to say the Extramagus's other target this time is Kimiko Ichiro. Nox burned their debt to her for this next part, so you better pay attention. They said that if you don't start communicating and cooperating with each other, you're both dead."

"But she broke into Mother's—"

"I don't care what she's gotten herself into."

"But he just threatened—"

"Honey Badger don't care, and neither does Alpha Wolf. Cut the crap, shoot the breeze, stay alive." I heard a long sigh. "Blaine, you tell her everything we've got. No matter what you think of her or what she might be doing in your house, Kim saved my life. She's a target now, and I owe her. You're paying it back for me. Nox and I will try to make it to your place by tomorrow."

"Don't bother." I blew a long stream of thinner smoke out my nose. "Mother's not letting anyone in except for the Head-mistress, Mr. Waban, and the Queen. She'd just tell you guys to scram."

"Okay, then. Maybe Ren can get in with the Queen's entourage, then."

"No!" Kimiko was on her feet, but she sat back down right away when I glared at her. "I mean, Ren's busy. He's got some important family stuff going on. Don't ask him to do anything else, I beg you."

"The only other packmate in the state is Tony," Josh grumbled. "Not the most reliable, but maybe he'll help. Talk to him."

"I did. Cat-man's doing what he can already."

"Oh. Wow, so something already happened?"

"Just bad luck." I shook my head, not wanting to go into the details of my sluggish clumsiness since coming back home for Spring Break. "Little things."

"Little things that add up to big." I was about to interrupt Kimiko, but she didn't talk about my tumble in the hall or anything embarrassing. Instead, she told him about how she'd checked our Luck, and it had turned. "Anyway, I'll help. Just send what you have to my phone. There just happens to be an app for that."

"Yup. It sounds like it might be coincidence again. You two be careful. Together. Take care of each other."

Josh hung up before we could protest. I led Kimiko out the door and back down the hall to her room in silence. She didn't speak, just looked up at me with those eyes, pupils dilated normally now. I reached out a hand to her, intending I don't even know what. She shouldn't want me to touch her after I exploded at her. I let it drop, but she caught it, gave it a squeeze with a steely grip I didn't expect.

"Together, like he said." She opened the door with her other hand, only letting go as she shut it. She hadn't averted her gaze or even blinked either, letting the panel of reinforced wood break our eye contact instead.

I stood outside for longer than I should have. When I finally turned to head back to my own room, a thick stalk of decorative bamboo in an urn crackled lightly.

"You'd better stay away from her, or I'll singe you and toss you into the Bay. She's my prisoner, not yours or your Queen's." I let the disguised Brownie quiver and headed back into my room to send all the Extramagus info to Kimiko. At least I wouldn't have to worry about her getting bored enough to climb out a window again. She'd have plenty to do.

Tony's PLEXIS Nexus search turned up a garden-variety Fire Magus, Richard Hopewell, who'd been married to Henrietta Thurston from the mid-1980s until just a few years ago. My fingers itched. I wanted to do another search, but couldn't without the login. I messaged the Shady Neighborhood Cat-man, asking him to search for Richard Hopewell's primary school and apprenticeship records from before the Reveal, also to do a search for Edgar Watkins. But Tony didn't answer. I zoned out to Angry Birds for so long I had to scramble to get ready in time to leave for dinner.

CHAPTER EIGHT

Kimiko

I didn't worry about the perfect dress anymore. The ones in the closet were all pretty close at any rate. I still couldn't figure out how they seemed meant for me or who put them in there on the same night I got stuck at the Harcourt mansion. I didn't have time to think about that now, anyway. Blaine and his friends were involved in something big, judging from the time it took to download the files he'd sent.

I clicked to open LORA, the Lucky analysis app I'd created while bored at the Academy, then spent the next hour letting it upload facts from Blaine's reports. Then, I pinned my hair up and took another shower while I waited. I wasn't the kind of girl who didn't break a sweat while hanging from a balcony and dealing with Blaine's dragon aggro.

"LORA, list the most common factors in the case."

The app followed my voice command, popping up three things immediately. First of all, the coincidence changes happened to exactly two people every time. Second, all the incidents occurred in Rhode Island. And third, multiple forms of magic were involved. That pointed to an Extramagus, like Josh said on the phone. But in all the reports, no one had figured out what the Extramagus's limitation was. I had a few possibilities, thanks to LORA. At least I'd have something to tell Blaine. But there had to be more.

"Check identities of Extramagi in the files against external sources." I let LORA chew on that while I went to the closet. At least I didn't have to check the weather after hanging out the window.

I slid hangers along the rod, flipping through dresses like pages in a paperback novel. I tried to care, but couldn't think straight. Extramagi were serious business, and one of them was after Blaine and me. I turned to the other side of the closet, hoping to find an outfit with pants. No such luck. Either whoever filled this wardrobe could fight in skirts, or they wanted to keep me from fighting. I went practical, selecting a vintage-looking style with a full knee-length skirt. It was yellow with gold threading along the hems, sleeves, and collar. The only shoes that matched had those stupid kitten heels, also known as ankle breakers.

But I could outwit the Harcourt Family Fashion Police. There were some flat patent turquoise Mary-Janes and a matching clutch. I grabbed those and found a filmy blue scarf to hang around the collar of a woolen camel coat. It was perfect, an outfit that couldn't possibly tempt Luck gone bad with a heel breaking, a purse strap catching on my neck, or a skirt tripping me up or hobbling me. And everything I wanted to bring would fit in the clutch, too.

I checked LORA again and found too large a list. I smacked my head and narrowed the parameters to Rhode Island. Stanhope, Edgewood, Williams. Of course, the oldest families. I scrolled down to see one more. Thurston. But the last recorded

Extramagus in that family had been back in Colonial times. Still, it was interesting. Blaine's report only mentioned the Stanhopes. I wondered whether that was bias. The PPC students seemed to genuinely like their Headmistress. Then again, it could be something more sinister. If I were head of a college and belonged to a family of Extramagi, I might try to remove the records from school resources.

But I'd seen Miss Thurston myself just that day. She didn't look like she had the energy to do much of anything, let alone keep the facts straight enough to lie like that. The thing about lying is you need to memorize the truth if you expect to do your falsehoods justice. Wise men say a lie with a grain of truth is more potent, but that's just a bunch of pretty words.

The truth is the rock you build your tower of lies on. If you don't know where the high tide stops, or whether that rock has a crack in it, that tower crashes down with you inside. The truth is a foundation, not something to ignore if you're the type of person who relies on embellishment. No, Henrietta Thurston wasn't in this, at least not intentionally.

LORA's next trick would take the rest of the night. I set my questions up, narrowing parameters to include only Rhode Island again and drank the rest of the tea on the food cart. After that, I put on some makeup and read through Blaine's reports from Fall Semester exam week when all this had apparently started. After reading for a while, I knew better.

Blaine blinked when I opened the door, shook his head, blinked again. The faint trail of smoke rising from his nose stopped cold. I stared. His eyes weren't narrowed, and his hair wasn't tied back, tangled, and dull. Instead, it hung just past his shoulders in chestnut waves I hadn't expected. He cleared his throat, then held out his arm. I reached for it, remembering the first time I'd been at the carousel in Roger Williams Park and managed to grab the ring. But Blaine wasn't a prize. He was a puzzle, a powerful ally or a dire enemy, depending on which way I tried to piece together my perception of him. Was his paranoia sea or sky, his bad Luck turn flora or fauna?

I kept pace with him down the hall. It was easy, even for someone as short as me. All I had to do was take two steps to each of his. Simple adaptation. Maybe that kind of thing doesn't come naturally to other people. I'll never know and don't really care because I'm me and perfectly fine with that.

Blaine turned left when I expected him to continue toward the back stairwell. Moments later, we stood at the top of a staircase swooping down from the third to the first floor like a pair of wings. An instant of vertigo and déjà vu threatened to overwhelm me. I felt I'd been here before, and under less pleasant circumstances for some reason. If it hadn't been for my hand on Blaine's arm, I might have found myself with my hand in his pocket, nicking his wallet. I also might have tumbled headfirst down the steps. Instead, I glanced to the side and up, my lips tilting to match what my eyes were doing.

Light flashed to my left and down. Gomer stood behind a tripod, wearing an unspoken apology on his wrinkled brow. So, Mrs. Harcourt approved of this little outing. I still had no idea why Blaine had decided to stick with the plan and take me out on the town, especially after the nastiness in his room earlier. I suspected he needed to get away from Mommie Dearest for some reason. The anti-spyware devices I'd seen in his room only supported that theory. Paranoid dragons were paranoid.

We made it down the stairs without any more weirdness. Mrs. Harcourt wasn't around, even though she'd clearly ordered her Goblin chef to record the momentous occasion of her son going out on an actual date. Gomer took another snapshot. Blaine cleared his throat instead of rolling his eyes, giving me the impression that this whole series of events was atypical. Once we were out the door, his arm relaxed, though he didn't shake off my grasp or change the angle of his elbow to make holding on awkward.

"Tiamat's Scales, I'm glad to be out of there." He let the chauffeur open the door for us but helped me into the car himself. "I can't believe Mother made Gomer break out the old camera."

"Does she do that every time you take a girl on a date?"

"I don't know." He settled in the seat across from me, his eyes fixed on my face.

"I don't understand." I did. He either hadn't taken a girl on a date before or not where his mother could have anything to do with it. I suspected Dad would have been challenging my dates to duels instead of snapping photos.

"I don't either." He puffed out a couple of smoke rings.

"So, why are we going?"

"Mostly, I needed to talk to friends from school this afternoon without you watching." His eyes made like little stars. "But that was then, this is now. Can't work together unless you're reading over my shoulder." He shrugged. "What did you think of the reports?"

"You and your friends have an entirely ineffective system for data analysis."

"Excuse me?" And there were those narrowed eyes I'd come to expect.

"Look, I'm not putting down your research. That's brilliant. It's the putting it together part I think needs work." I pulled out my phone. "I used this app, put your data into it. It's analyzing something now, but you can check the previous results."

He took the phone, swiping and tapping through the stuff I'd found out earlier. He blinked, shaking his head again like he did back in front of my door.

"Who did you steal this software from?" Blaine winked before I could slap him.

"I coded it."

"Wow. You're a coder?"

"It's a hobby. The Academy doesn't have much to do besides super easy homework." I shrugged. "You're lucky."

"Huh?"

"Getting into PPC." The laugh I intended came out more like a whimper. "I didn't have the grades."

"That's not luck, it's hard work." The words dropped out of his mouth like a bag of chips from a vending machine.

"Is that something you believe, or more programming from the Mom unit?" I didn't actually try to stop my eyebrow from gaining altitude, but maybe I should have.

"Look, no one gets away with insulting Mother. Not even me." He shook his head, then raised his chin. "But I guess a Luck expert would be able to properly question philosophies on blanket Luck statements. My grades are mine, not Mother's. Those came from busting my tail, and I won't let you tell me otherwise, Tanuki or no."

"People make Luck, you know. If Extrahumans like you didn't, there wouldn't even be Luck charms."

"And Josh wouldn't be here. Point taken." He actually smiled. I closed my eyes, unable to watch his relief at the event I'd doomed my father with. "Hey." Fabric rustled. His hand covered mine. The car stopped, and he pulled it away.

I could have just sat in that car for a few hours, forced Blaine to take me back to the mansion and haul me inside. Instead, I opened my eyes when the chauffeur opened the door. I got out like a good little date and stood at the curb as the car pulled away. Blaine took my hand this time instead of offering his arm, leading me slowly through a small park.

"What happened back in the car?"

"I just got reminded of something."

"Anything you need help with?"

"Wait." I tugged on his hand, stopping him. He turned. "You

want to know why I broke in. This thing that's got me down. It's the reason."

"And it has something to do with Josh Dennison."

"So you know. You knew all this time?"

"I know nothing, Kimiko." He squeezed my hand. "I deduce."

"Well, do you still want to offer me help when you don't even know what my problem is?"

"I do. Whether I can or not is another story. Some tall orders are big as houses. Others are Mount Everest."

"I'm still not sure I should tell you, or anyone else." I sniffed, hoping he'd think it was allergies. I shut my eyes.

"I get it. You're used to doing everything for yourself. 'If you want something done right' and all that?"

"Yeah."

"Come on, then." He put an arm around my shoulders. "We can talk about it when you absolutely have to." I shivered, but definitely not with cold. Blaine Harcourt was driving me crazy, one minute all smoke and angst, the next a chivalry most would expect from knights instead of dragons.

I hadn't seen a fraction of that yet as it turned out.

CHAPTER NINE

Blaine

I might not know why, but Kimiko Ichiro needed a Luck charm. And I wanted to help her, but Mother let nothing leave her hoard without some dangerous bargain or ironclad agreement. Then again, she'd given me the task of resolving Kimiko's break-in. Tanuki only needed Luck charms for life-saving magic, so if she was trying to steal one, it could mean someone was in mortal danger. But she was a consummate liar. I couldn't fault her for it, though, considering that was one of my own talents. I'd come to an understanding. She angered me so much because of what we had in common. Unexpected mirrors were startling.

While kicking myself for wasting time casually gaming instead of pinging Tony for advice on outwitting a Tanuki, I realized all I should do is figure out what I would do in her situation. I kept my arm around her as I walked through and out of the park and then down Memorial Boulevard. The streets were quiet, almost empty. Lights were on at the bed-and-breakfast up ahead.

As we crossed the side-street and approached the converted Victorian house, a woman dashed down the steps. She tripped the contents of her pink suitcase spilling on the sidewalk in front of us. What I could see of her face behind strands of blonde hair reddened. I knew her.

"Jeannie?" I held out a hand to help her up. "Jeannie La Montagne?" The bear shifter was also a Resident Assistant at the PPC dorms.

"Ugh. It figures I'd run into someone I know on the worst night of my adult life." She brushed her hair off her face. Tears streaked mascara in trails down her cheeks.

"Are you okay?" Kimiko got down on the sidewalk, collecting items and stuffing them back in the suitcase. I watched her. No sleight-of-hand. "What happened?"

"Well, I kind of got stranded here unexpectedly." She sighed, looking like the last thing she wanted to do was talk about it. But then, a man stepped out on the porch.

"Jeannie, come on. Come back inside, and we'll talk about this."

"No way, Dale. Stay here alone or with your side piece for all I care." Jeannie snatched a can of hairspray out of Kimiko's hand and flung it at Dale. He ducked, and it hit the wall.

"She meant nothing to me."

"It would be better if she did." Jeannie's throat rumbled with a low growl.

"Woah." Dale paled. I would too if I was a regular guy with a jilted bear-shifter girlfriend.

Jeannie's pert nose darkened as she began shifting. She turned her head, looking away from Dale and out somewhere toward the street. Messenger on my phone beeped, then I heard a moped in the distance. A black sedan turned from the intersection we'd just crossed, the heavily tinted window opened a crack. I smelled oil and gunpowder. Kimiko stared at Jeannie, completely oblivious.

My skin scaled over and the seams at the back of my jacket popped. I took one step back and over to put myself between the car and Kimiko. My partially shifted wings opened, circling around her. The engine revved, and then the bullets hit.

Scales are slightly better than kevlar for stopping mundane bullets, but the semi-automatic rounds felt like that one time I'd flown in a hailstorm. The rain of pain stayed mainly on the Blaine. None of them touched Kimiko or Jeannie. Dale jumped, then ducked back inside. Slugs hit the steps, chewing holes through the wood like giant metallic carpenter ants on speed. Chips flew up from the sidewalk, bouncing off my wingtips. I stared at Kimiko as though I could will her to stay still. She trembled, covering her ears.

A roar and the screech of claws on metal made me lower the clear protective lid on my eyes to turn my head. A massive golden bear tore the rear bumper off the car. Jeannie. She bellowed again, and I heard the car's engine whine. The driver floored it harder, tires squealing in their bid for traction against damp pavement. It fishtailed, and part of me hoped it'd flip. It didn't. Instead, the sedan scurried down the street, its back end wiggling like a *cucaracha* escaping a descending shoe.

A few deep breaths and some concentration had my wings folded against my back and scales fading from red to beige. I shifted back to almost human but left my skin armored except for my palms and fingertips. I pulled my phone from my pocket, thankful to have left it in a front pocket instead of the back. There was a message from Tony.

Goombas

The moped I'd heard before the attack chugged by, a familiar trench coat flapping behind the driver. That damn cat. He'd been following the shooters, referred to them as Goombas in our messages that afternoon. That could only mean one thing.

"How did you manage to piss off the Gatto Gang?" Jeannie spoke to Kimiko, who'd just given the bear shifter her coat.

"No idea." She shivered again. Or maybe she hadn't stopped. "They hate my dad, though. You know those offers they say you can't refuse?"

"Yeah?" Police sirens dragged out behind her question.

"Well, my dad did refuse them. More than once."

"Ugh." Jeannie pulled mismatched clothes from her bullet-riddled suitcase and pulled them on. "Well, those particular guys won't be messing with you again tonight."

Red and blue lights swirled and strobed, making the primary color trifecta on this corner of Memorial Drive. We waited, letting the staff members at the Bed and Breakfast give official statements to the uniformed officers on the scene.

"What's up, dude?" A detective in a puffy orange vest and acid-wash jeans flashed his badge and a set of fangs. His partner rolled her eyes, then focused a blue steel glare right at Jeannie.

"Um, not much. Do you want me to fill out a form or something, Detective…"

"Klein. Naw, dude." The detective shook his head, then turned to glance at his partner. His mullet would have put MacGyver's to shame. "I want you to answer my partner's questions." He waved a hand in her direction. "Detective Weaver."

"Okay." I turned to face the much scarier looking of the two. Her hair was highly polished, held up in a clip at the back of her head. It shone with some kind of immobilizing styling product, looking almost bullet-proof. One thick streak of white stood out in the otherwise conservative dark brown hair. A faint scar marked the expanse of forehead under the streak. My nose twitched, and I blinked my still active inner lid. The scary detective was some kind of shifter, but not one of the magical type. She also had a hint of Psychic power around her. A device? Her clothes? I glanced at Klein again. Not a trace of any Psychic energy on him. I smiled at scary streak lady.

"Can you identify the shooter?" Her face was deader-pan than Ben Stein's voice.

"Nope, sorry." I shrugged. She stared at me without blinking.

"What if I told you we saw someone in the area we know you are acquainted with?"

"Yeah. Tony Gitano." I nodded. "I saw him, but he had nothing to do with this."

"Are you sure?" I wasn't sure how Detective Meat Cleaver Weaver managed to keep her eyes open without them tearing.

"Look, Tony's not my favorite person in the world, but he couldn't have been shooting at me from that sedan." I waved my hand. "He putt-putted by on a Vespa like the lamest excuse for Ghost Rider in the known universe."

Detective Klein chuckled. His partner snapped her fingers, and he stopped it on a dime. I wiped the smirk off my face. Apparently, any charm or wit was lost on Detective Weaver. I straightened my tie, and what was left of my shirt, trying to imagine I was talking to Mother. The last thing I wanted was to get taken down to the station for questioning, and this felt like some kind of test.

"We've been watching you, Harcourt." The detective pointed one claw-like finger at my chest. "You or any of your little friends make one wrong move here in Newport, and we're on you like spiders on flies."

"Yes, ma'am." I gulped. She nodded, apparently mollified for the time being.

"I got their statements." Detective Klein waved a couple of triplicate sheets marked with Kimiko's and Jeannie's names in the air.

Detective Weaver didn't say anything. Her face could have been on one of the marble statues in Mother's poison apple grove. She turned her back and stalked off to her car, Detective Klein following at a safe distance. What in the name of Tiamat could she be? I held my breath until they got in their unmarked sedan and pulled away.

"Creepy spider shifters you have on the police force here."

Kimiko patted my arm. "I'm sorry. Not apologetically, but in the sympathy kind of way."

"So that's what she was. Spider shifter." I shuddered. Spiders freaked me out almost as much as Pharaoh's Rats. Tiny things were more dangerous to dragons than other dragons most of the time.

"Well, the big bad spider's gone now." Kimiko winked. "Why not head off to wherever we were going as long as we'll make it in time for the reservation?"

"Um, but I'm not really dressed for that anymore." I turned my back, letting Kimiko and Jeannie inspect my shredded jacket and the holes in my shirt. Even though my dress shirts had special flaps to accommodate my wings in an emergency, the bullets had done a number on it.

"It's not really that bad. Mostly, you'll need a jacket." Jeannie's voice came from behind me as she plucked at my shirt. "They have those at most restaurants here, for people who show up too touristy." She stepped back around in front of me, standing next to Kimiko.

"Yeah, I guess you're right." I sighed. "Still, Mother's going to hear about this, and she wouldn't want me to go ahead with dinner after a drive-by."

Jeannie nodded, of course. She was an RA after all, the kind of person used to passing the buck and respecting the sort of authority my mother represented. Kimiko raised an eyebrow, shaking her head. One of her turquoise-shod toes tapped the pavement.

"You mean to tell me you've been stuck in that house for half a week and you're going home just because some assholes who won't come back shot at your scaly ass?" She twirled her hair. "Well, if that's what Mother thinks is best, I guess you ought to do it, right?"

The zing of sarcasm under her words made me tingle all over. I blinked my clear lid, looking for anything out of the ordinary about her energy. Nothing. But the entire idea she'd presented, rebellion against the great and powerful Hertha Harcourt, apex dragon shifter of the Eastern Seaboard, hit me with more force than all the Gatto Gang's bullets. A west wind blew around me, brushing her bangs aside. I noticed the tiny star-shaped scar again, focused on it. It was paler than the rest of her skin, clearly old. I wondered again where had I seen something like that before.

"You're right." I took a step toward her, reaching one hand out, not entirely sure what I was about to do. Jeannie cleared her throat.

"Now that I'm a third wheel dressed in Flasher Couture, I'd better get to the bus station and hope no one calls the cops before they open in the morning."

"Wait, Jeannie." I turned, my hand still extended. I flattened my palm into an inclusive gesture. "You're always getting us out of trouble back on campus. The least I can do is pull a string and get you a smarmy ex-boyfriend free place to stay. Come on."

Jeannie nodded and said something, but I barely noticed. Kimiko gazed up at me like I was some kind of hero even though Jeannie had actually run the bad guys off. But that look on her face wasn't about the drive-by, or was it? It didn't really matter. What did was that girls didn't look at me like that. I was always the brainy buddy or the smart-aleck sidekick, or the also-ran rival to any women of substance.

I was the guy shallow girls brought home for kicks, not to their families. I recited a litany in my head about her mysterious break-in, her lies, her sticky fingers, the poison apple. She walked along next to me, so close our hands kept touching. I shut the litany off and put my arm around her again. She was my problem in so many ways already, what was one more?

We walked the rest of the way to the Spiced Bear, which was inside a swankier place to stay than the one Jeannie's cheating ex-boyfriend had booked for them. I got her a room, and she went up to it. We were just in time for our reservation. And of course, the restaurant had a tatty tweed they kept for vacationers who'd forgotten the jackets-required policy. It reminded me of Professor Watkins. As we sat down, I remembered all the information Kimiko's app had organized. It'd have to wait for another minute or three, though.

"Um, they're going to come over here to take our wine order, and I don't know whether—"

"I'm old enough to drink, Blaine." She winked. I imagined having wine and other things with her in an extremely unorthodox and messy fashion. I was so distracted I didn't notice the hostess standing at my elbow with the telephone.

"Sir, a call for you."

"No, thanks." I waved her away.

"But, sir, She insisted." The capital letter in her voice meant it was Mother on the line.

"That's lovely of her. Please tell her I'm handling the situation, per her orders." I smiled. "We would like a bottle of Cardinale. And we'll have my usual for dinner. Thanks."

"Very good, sir." The hostess gave a slight bow and carried the phone away.

The meal was phenomenal as usual, and the company matched. But the best part of all was knowing I was having dinner here tonight by my own choice, not Mother's. I'd been around more than one block in the physical sense with women, but this was different. I wasn't out on a date with Kimiko Ichiro because I could be, or because Mother wanted me to be. We sat in the Spiced Bear because we wanted to be there together, and that made more of a difference than I could ever have imagined it would.

We didn't have time to walk after dinner. So we kept the meal-time conversation light, focusing on the games we hadn't played earlier that day. After getting my scales filled with lead, I deserved to relax and have fun. Kimiko seemed to understand that didn't happen too often for me, or maybe she felt the same way. Lockdown at The Academy trapped her as surely as expectations and obligations caged me. But she'd gotten out of that prison. I could bust out of mine, too. She helped me see how when you break free once, you learn to watch the exits just in case you need one the next time.

The limo stood at the curb directly in front of the steps, and we got inside and let the driver take us back to the mansion. This time, I sat next to her instead of across. She turned, looking at me expectantly. But I couldn't put my arm around her like I had on the relatively anonymous streets. Going back home was like going back into battle after a respite. When she put her hand over mine, I should have shaken it off. I didn't.

When we got out of the car, Mother was waiting. She gave me a smile that glittered like fool's gold. I wanted to look back, give whichever servant assigned to escort Kimiko back to her room a little stink-eye motivation to leave me to it. Mother wasn't having any of that. She had her game face on. When she stalked up the staircase and turned left, I knew she meant to give me five kinds of nastiness, all in the spirit of Tiamat's five heads. I followed, clenching my fists.

I wasn't surprised when she brought me to her rage cage. She'd spent too much time lately in the saltine-box shaped room, lined in granite from floor to ceiling. This was where Mother always went when she thought her temper needed a release. The only decor was what appeared to be wall carvings, vaguely runic. I knew better. The whole chamber was big enough for four fully shifted dragons and warded more heavily than some prisons. She waved a hand, and the door closed behind me. I knew this drill well. I wouldn't be leaving until she either opened that door or conceded to any argument I might present.

"How dare you disobey your mother?" She put all her weight on one leg and crossed her arms over her chest.

"Are you serious, Mother?" I'd been shot at, interrogated by a spider shifter, and rescued two people. I would not just stand there and eat the helping of Guilt Trip Supreme she wanted to dish out.

"Deadly." She tossed her head, black hair falling behind her shoulder on the right.

"That's interesting because you're the one who wanted me to write the story of Kimiko Ichiro and the Mysterious Dragon Hoard Invasion." I narrowed my eyes, homing in on the corners of her mouth and her nostrils. That's where she wore all her human form tells. "I was handling that."

"You'd just been shot at. Why in Tiamat's name would you go out and have a leisurely dinner afterward?"

"To get the girl I shielded from gunfire and certain death to talk to me, of course." I rolled my eyes, but only after a pause. I hoped she didn't notice my own slip in the Tells You Don't Show And Expect To Win At Poker department. "It's a tactic I learned from the best."

"You haven't used what you've learned by watching me before. Why start now?"

"You haven't dropped a responsibility this big and important in my lap before. Why start now?"

Her only response was a low growl. Someone who'd never lived with her may have mistaken it for a warning or expression of anger. I didn't. I ducked. Good thing.

The hiss behind me meant Mother's acid breath was doing the Alka Seltzer Sizzle on solid rock. From experience, I knew that if she hit me, I wouldn't heal for days. The wall wouldn't heal at all, though. I didn't bother looking over my shoulder because I knew there'd be one more vaguely runic line etched back there. I straightened, mirroring her cross-armed pose.

"Don't question my judgment, whelp, until you're prepared to challenge me for this estate and everything in it."

"And how do you know I'm not?"

"Because even you have no idea exactly what and who will become your responsibility if you do." Mother tapped the toe of one five-figure price-tag shoe against the stone.

"A point that becomes more irrelevant every time we have an argument like this." My dagger-thin glare turned into more of a squint as the smoke rising from my nostrils thickened. "Be careful, or all the trouble you went to, using nurture to direct me away from Father's mistakes, will backfire. Literally." I took a deep breath.

One corner of her matte-red mouth twitched down, and her weight shifted to her other leg. I let the breath out with a laugh instead of the gout of flame she must have expected. Although Mother stood up straight after that and put on her most withering glare, she seemed smaller than usual, somehow.

"You don't know what you're talking about." Nothing moved besides her mouth. "Until you understand the full extent of what you're inheriting, you will never be ready to."

"Like you were ready when it happened for you?" I put my hands on my hips.

"You are not me." Her eyes shifted from round pupils to slitted, dark brown to poison-green.

"Good."

"I already know how you feel about that, and now it's time for you to understand that I agree." She closed her inner eyelid. "No one should have to do the things I've done, especially not you. And that's why I say again, you are not ready to inherit everything in this house, whether you do it by challenging me or some other way."

"You aren't having me investigate Kimiko because of any

danger she presents." I tightened my grip on my own arms instinctively. "You're worried about something else." I blinked. "Some*one* else."

Mother didn't answer. Instead, she turned her back, walking slow and steady toward the windowless end of the room. Before she disappeared into the dim and cavernous end of the room, she waved one hand. The door unlocked, and stone ground against steel as it opened.

I'd won the argument but lost something else. The shield of feigned ignorance.

CHAPTER TEN

Kimiko

At the door, Gomer waited to escort me via the back stairs to my room while Blaine went up the showy staircase with Mrs. Harcourt. Usually, eavesdropping was one of my favorite pastimes. The thought of listening in on whatever chewing-out Blaine would get made me vaguely ill.

I ran the bath again, stepping out of the shoes and the dress. The contents of the turquoise clutch went back in my own handbag, locked in the drawer again. A search of the drawers didn't turn up anything like the cozy flannel pajamas I would have put on back home after a night like this. So I selected a raw silk nightgown in dusky pink and hung it on a hook in the bathroom. I would enter the data about the shooting and try talking to Ismail after my bath.

I'd fallen asleep in the tub. A knock on the bathroom door startled me out of the tepid water. I toweled off quickly, then slipped the nightgown on and opened the door. Instead of the

Brownie or Gomer, or even Ismail, it was Blaine. He'd changed his pants but had no shirt on. His skin was smooth, no hint of scales. It was also flawless, like his well-defined muscles. I hadn't imagined a bookwyrm would look so manly without a shirt, dragon shifter or no.

"How did you get in?" I glanced past him, rubbing my arms at an unexpected chill in the air.

"Nature's hang-glider." He jerked his chin at the balcony doors. "Much safer than your Spider Kim act."

"Yeah." I brushed past him to grab the bathrobe I'd left on the bed, and our arms touching sent a shiver across my skin and a heated flush up from my center. I wasn't cold anymore, but I put the bathrobe on, anyway. "What did you come here for?" I couldn't look at him when I said it and fiddled with the key on its chain instead.

"That LORA app…you said it was running something." His gaze bounced around the room, alighting just about everywhere except on me.

"Oh." I shouldn't have been disappointed. "Okay." I headed to the nightstand, shielded it with my body, and reached in for my phone. I needn't have bothered. Blaine wasn't looking. I stepped in front of him, clasping the phone in my hands between us. "Um, can I ask you something?"

"Um, yeah. You just did." He smirked, finally meeting my gaze. He put his hands in his pockets. "But you can ask something else."

"You're supposed to find out why I'm here, and how I broke in." I took a deep breath, feeling like I was about to step off a cliff or out of a plane and plummet to my death. "And I just opened a locked drawer in front of you. You didn't try to peek. Why?"

"Because you were going to tell me something back at the park." Blaine pulled his hands out of his pockets and opened one, revealing a small black orb on a silver chain. He touched it, setting it alight with some kind of Extrahuman energy. Then he looped the chain over his wrist and held out his hand. I took the hint, let go of the phone, and put one of my hands in, too. He clasped my hand and gazed into my eyes. The tingle I felt had nothing to do with magic. "You can tell me now without anyone overhearing."

"It's my dad. He's got maybe a week to live without a Luck charm." I closed my eyes. "And your mother's the only person in this hemisphere who has any."

"So you thought pissing off a dragon family was the way to go?" Smoke billowed from his nose and mouth, making me feel like I was in the belly of an impending thunderstorm. "Assumed I'm just like Mother and any other textbook dragon, even after what I did for Nox. I mean, come on. You were there. I got Mother to give up a pelt, but Josh almost died. And you. Don't. Bother. To. Ask." His hand gripped mine tighter, and the heat of his breath was like a furnace on my cheek as I tried not to quake in fear. I opened my eyes. But Blaine didn't look angry. His shoulders were too droopy for that.

"It's my fault, Blaine." I looked the dragon right in the eyes, wishing I could flame up like the extinct Phoenix and match the inferno of whatever emotion fueled his fire. All I got for my trouble was a torrent of tears rolling down my face. "If I hadn't swiped Dad's pin and used it on Josh, he'd be fine. It was his last Luck charm. If I can't get him another one, I've killed my own father, just because I'm a kleptomaniac who thought Luck was on her side."

Blaine blinked, his grip loosening. He reached out to brush my tears away, and I flinched at the heat coming from him. The tears evaporated before his hand made contact with my cheek. He took a deep breath, lowering the temperature around us by at least three degrees. Then, he took another, closing his eyes. When he opened them, they were ember-red and reptilian.

"You did no such thing." He pulled me closer, holding me against his chest as I shook and wept. "It's the Extramagus. Coincidence. You're the one who said our Luck's turned. I just checked, and our magic energy's all over the place. We're a mess, Kimiko, because some asshole has a vendetta against desegregating Providence Paranormal College. Not because you saved a life. And you couldn't have known ahead of time that was your father's last charm."

I couldn't say anything to that. He was right. Blaine just gave me the benefit of the doubt about the charm. His confidence in me was a bigger mystery than anything I'd ever encountered. I didn't dare look up at him;. My face had to be a puffy mess from the ugly crying that went with my confession. But I couldn't stay like that, melting against his bare chest in a more figurative sense than his earlier temperature might have meant.

Blaine pulled back, easing my face off his shoulder. He gazed down at me, his eyes that amber-brown again. My knees felt weak, and my lower lip trembled. His face bent closer to mine until our lips almost touched. We both turned our heads at the wooden crackling sound from the corner.

"Fewmets!" He let go of me, pulling the anti-spyware amulet off my wrist as he headed toward the decorative bamboo in the golden urn. He pulled back his arm, making a fist.

"No!" I ran up behind him, leaping up to drag down his elbow.

Blaine's punch went wide, colliding with the mirrored wall instead of the Brownie hiding with the decor. A spiderweb of cracks appeared on the fake glass, extending all the way up to the ceiling. That was one camera in the room down for the count.

"Why are you stopping me from taking out a spy?" Blaine's nostrils flared, smoke puffing out in a thin curl. The tilt of his head and his tone of voice told me he'd reined his anger in, waiting for a real answer.

"Are you sure they're not an ally?"

"Point." He reached out, grasping the Brownie with one hand and pulling them from the urn. Gold powder dusted his palm when he let them go. The natural muddy brown of their bark showed through their disguise. "But we can't question them without getting in their debt."

"They'll want to come out of this unscathed, though." I turned my head to look at the Brownie. "They'll tell us something on their own if they know what's best, and Brownies are supposed to be canny."

"I am." The Brownie's creaky voice was nearly lost in the rattle they made as they bent toward one of the concealed cameras.

"This has those taken care of." Blaine held up the amulet. "So give me a reason not to turn you into firewood."

"Your mother doesn't employ my kind. I'm not here to spy for your enemy."

"Go on." Smoke wafted toward the wooden creature with Blaine's words.

"I can't tell you who sent me or why. Prior agreement." The Brownie crackled again. "All I can tell you is, my debtor is your ally."

"Of course." He rolled his eyes, then offered me his arm. "Still, there are some things that just aren't anyone's business, not even some mysterious benefactor's." Blaine turned to face me, smirking. "Would you like to make a bit of a scene, Kimiko? I promise it's all in the interest of getting to the bottom of this predicament."

"Um, sure?" I took his arm more out of desire to touch him again than anything else, although curiosity was a close second. The feel of his skin under my hand was downright addictive. I took a deep breath as he walked me to the door. He dropped his arm, wrapping it around my waist.

"Prepare to meet a pretend scoundrel. I solemnly swear I'm not up to no good, but you ought to act like I am, anyway." I tittered in response. Blaine's wit was as quick as mine. The swoon I faked at him was more genuine than I wanted to admit.

I turned my laughter into an indignant shriek when Blaine

kicked the door to my room open and slung me over his shoulder. I watched from my upside-down position as he hip-checked the door shut. He stormed down the hall, more smoke than I'd ever seen trailing over his head and behind him. A low growl in his throat underscored my shrieks.

"You infuriating woman." Blaine's voice was a strained snarl. I could imagine the sneer curling his upper lip. "You're mine, you hear me? Mine to deal with as I see fit. Yes, I'm entitled. You're just a thieving Tanuki at my mercy. You will do as I say."

I cased the hallway, realizing he was putting on a show for the audio and visual recording devices spaced at regular intervals. I let myself tremble and whimper, knowing that whoever monitored those feeds would have no idea all my fuss came from a giggle fit instead of abject terror. A few tears rolled over my forehead, meeting the marble floors with soft plops. Only a Memory Psychic would be able to tell those came from the biggest laugh of the year and not Blaine's snarly threats.

We kept it up all the way to the end of the hall and through the outward swing of the door, the slam of it shutting, and the bolt being thrown.

After that, Blaine dropped me on the foot of his bed and collapsed on a little bench in front of it, clutching his sides. It took several minutes for me to catch my breath or remember that he'd carried me over his shoulder in nothing but a flimsy nightgown.

CHAPTER ELEVEN

Blaine

Making a truckload of smoke with Kimiko Ichiro over my shoulder: easy. Putting her down and letting her go afterward: nearly impossible. The bench creaked under me as I tumbled against it, not wanting to actually get on the bed with her. That was a crock of bull. I wanted nothing more than that but had told her the threats and the carrying on down the hall were all for show. When I gave my word, I kept it. There was no way a girl like her would want a pile of anxiety like me for anything but a fling. That near-miss kiss and the way she'd looked at me after the shooting could only be a flash-in-the-pan kind of thing. I wouldn't take advantage of a girl whose father was on borrowed time. I wouldn't even try courting her unless I could think of a way to help her first.

Before she composed herself, I got up and went through my audio surveillance negating routine. I wondered why Mother even bothered spying on me that way when I knew how to get around it so handily. Maybe she just had it set up in case anything happened in here while I was asleep. But that meant she thought someone in the house might be a danger to me. I shivered, suddenly chilled. It might just be paranoia. It sort of ran in dragonish families, after all, and I knew for sure I'd gotten a hefty dose of it myself. But just because you're paranoid doesn't mean someone's not out to get you.

And I knew for sure now. Kimiko Ichiro was not out to get my family or me. She was just dealing with the worst string of Luck a Tanuki could have encountered. If I thought Mother would believe me and let her go, I'd go tell her that instant. It'd never work. Mother had her jaws clamped around the idea that Kimiko's way in meant some heinous enemy could figure out how to break in and murderate the place. If she hadn't softened her paranoid stance during our after-dinner argument, she probably never would.

A bright guitar riff erupted from the speakers I'd placed around the room to achieve surround-sound. Oh, no, this was not the playlist I wanted to subject other people to. Before I could reach out to skip the embarrassingly outdated pop-punk music, Kimiko slapped my hand away. I blinked down at her smile.

"Leave it. This band is super corny, but I always loved this song." She grabbed my hands and pulled me back to the bench, swaying in time to the music as we went. Then she did the last thing I expected: she belted out every word of Simple Plan's *Addicted*. I sat down, watching her pick up a hairbrush and give an American Idol-worthy rendition for an audience of one.

"Did anyone ever tell you that you ought to do that kind of thing professionally?" She had one of those signature voices, the kind that wouldn't be mistaken for anyone else's. I hadn't been able to take my eyes off her the entire time. She'd nailed the song to my heart, mind, and attention span as blatantly as Martin Luther nailed his Ninety-Five Theses to the door of the

Castle Church. I was the most fervent kind of believer, a convert.

"Yeah." She put the hairbrush down. "Ren." She shrugged, then plopped down on the bench next to me. "I gave up after that car accident, though."

"Oh." I got up and started pacing—anything to keep away from her. I was addicted, all right, like the song said. And still a dick, although trying not to be a giant one. "Well, you should take it up again, now that it turns out he's alive after all."

"Love to, if I could find the time. Breaking out of the Academy and stalking my dad got pretty time-consuming, you know. So's this lovely stay in the Newport Mansion." Kimiko twisted the tithing bracelet on her wrist. "Anyway, don't we have some investigating to do?"

"Yeah." I headed over to my desk, grabbed a couple of tablets from the top drawer. I tossed one on the bed near her and fired up the other. "Can you load your LORA app on these?"

"Sure I can, but should I?" She tilted her head, making her hair fall away from her chest. The nightgown she wore had a plunging neckline. I looked away as fast as I could, straining something in my neck.

"Ow." I winced. My muscles started trying to knit back together around the stupid knot. I tried rubbing it, but the damn thing was on the back of my shoulder.

"Sit." She gestured to the floor in front of the bench.

I sat. Didn't have much choice. Stupid accidents like that sucked for shifters, especially any flying ones. If I didn't get the knot worked out, it could carry over when I shifted and mess with my wing on that side. I put my hands on the floor, tucking them under my legs. That'd force me to keep them to myself. I wish I could say her touch melted all the tension away, but it didn't. If anything, it got worse.

"You're super tense." Her fingers pressed against both my shoulders, which probably felt like concrete. She gave up trying to rub or even prod and started punching instead. I sighed, leaning back.

"Yeah. Been a rough couple days for both of us."

"Wow." Her fists beat harder. "So big lizards are capable of empathy. Who knew?"

"It's the big secret of my people. We care." I snorted a laugh past my gritted teeth. It hurt, but she was breaking down the knot. "Little Tanuki girls have magic punches. Who'd have thought?"

"No one. Being easily underestimated is all part of my charm." She took her hands away, and I failed at not whining about it. "Okay, LORA's loaded up on these. Data's synced, too."

"I hear he's also fully functional." There was no way she'd get that reference.

"And anatomically correct." She tapped my much more relaxed shoulder with the corner of one of the tablets. I turned around and instantly regretted it. Well, no, I didn't. I regretted my reaction to her legs at eye-level. Anatomically correct didn't begin to describe. Anatomically amazing, astounding and a million other adjectives raced through my brain, not necessarily in alphabetical order. Maybe. I don't really remember. All I know for sure was I couldn't stand up.

"Look, I'm having a hard time here. Focusing, I mean. On stuff."

"Oh?" Kimiko blinked wide eyes, but I knew better than to assume her innocence was anything but a facade. She had to be deliberately teasing me. It felt like my head would explode in more ways than one if you get my drift.

"Yeah. Look, I shouldn't have dragged you out of there before you could get decent."

"Maybe, maybe not. But you did." Her smile was gentler than I'd expected. She stepped down from the bench, joining me on the floor. She left the tablet up there, then plucked mine from my hands and set it on top of hers. I thought the innuendo in the gesture couldn't possibly be intentional. I. Thought. Wrong.

Before I could say anything, Kimiko was in my lap, arms around my neck and legs around my waist like she'd been in the vault. This time, she wasn't fighting me, though. She pressed her forehead against mine, the tips of our noses touched, and our breath mingled. She sat, waiting. I tilted my head until our lips met instead of our foreheads, and then everything changed.

It wasn't what you think. The kiss was barely a brush of our lips. Nothing else happened because I was swept away. A memory, tiny but bright, like a light at the end of a tunnel, grew closer as I rushed toward it. If I'd been on the PPC campus, I'd think I'd been whammied by one of Henry's memory amulets or something. But I knew that wasn't the case. Once I got to the corner of my mind the kiss had pushed me toward, I understood.

I recognized myself from old photographs. The nearly blond hair of my early childhood graced the top of my head, and I was dressed all in red, sitting across from a little brown-haired girl with furry ears wearing the same color. Gomer was there, knife poised over an undecorated cake. Mother's voice instructed me to hold hands with the girl, and then an invisible force wrapped a cord made of twisted paper around our wrists. We sat with our hands tied together like that, listening to a man's voice drone out a phrase in what I now recognized as bastardized Latin. Memory me glanced up, seeing only a rotund figure, face obscured in the shadow cast by his black Greek fisherman's hat. A sudden, sharp pain pricked the top center of my forehead and thin twin cries welled up shrilly from child-throats.

I shook my head, snapping myself out of it. Kimiko still sat in my lap, but her eyes were glassy and far away, still lost in the hidden memory our first kiss had returned. I studied her face, finally reaching out to brush aside her bangs. The tiny star-shaped scar there was familiar because it mirrored mine. I finally understood why Mother had passed the responsibility of dealing with our intruder to me, and why she seemed to approve of and even like our would-be burglar despite her actions.

Kimiko Ichiro was my betrothed, had been since we were barely out of diapers. I could have someone take the tithing bracelets off, but I'd be stuck with her forever. And it didn't matter one bit to either of our families whether or not we liked it.

CHAPTER TWELVE

Kimiko

Blaine Harcourt was my betrothed. And someone had erased our memories of the whole entire event. I opened my eyes to find myself in his arms, his face bent over mine. Blaine's eyes softened with concern, the amber-brown color reminding me of scotch. I reached up, touching the side of his face. My thumb strayed to the corner of his mouth and stopped. I felt my heart thud in my chest. Should I get so intimate with him right after finding something like that out? Maybe he wasn't okay with being betrothed in general, or maybe not to me in particular.

"Thank Tiamat you're okay." Blaine stood up, carrying me to a chaise in the corner near his desk. "I wasn't sure you'd come out of that trance on your own."

"Well, I did. Sucks to be you." I blinked. "What happened?"

"Memory suppression broke is my guess." Blaine sat at his desk, fingers hitting the keys on his laptop. "But I'm asking the expert right now."

"Expert?"

"Henry Baxter, Psychic vampire. He's a Memory Psychic and a student at PPC, so if there's some type of Magus who can take a memory like that and make it come back, he'd know about it."

"Wait, you think the guy in the hat was a Magus and not a Psychic, even after the conversation we overheard this morning?"

"Um." His fingers froze, hovering over the keyboard like a pair of umbrellas. "Huh. Good question, good point." He stood, cracked his knuckles, and paced a couple of times in front of the chaise. "It's just that, you know, when you've watched six of your friends go through near-death experiences at the hands of a mysterious Extramagus, you jump to conclusions."

"I understand. But Occam had a Razor, and he knew how to use it. Simpler is better. Doesn't it make sense that at least one of our parents wouldn't want us to remember we were betrothed until we were old enough to lip-lock on our own? Maybe our parents hired him."

"Oh, definitely. Thanks for pointing out my paranoia." He glanced back at the screen. "Ha! Are you a Ravenclaw or a Gryffindor?"

"Um, Slytherin." I rolled my eyes. "Duh."

"Oh. Well, nobody's perfect. I forgive you. Also, ten points to Slytherin!" Blaine chuckled. "Henry's a Hufflepuff, but he totally agrees with your idea. It's most likely a Psychic because Magi with that kind of power are extremely rare. Except, he says, it's got to be a master-Level psychic. Someone who'd be qualified to teach doctoral-level stuff at PPC. And he only knows of one person like that who was around back then. His old mentor."

"Awesome, so Henry can tell us if he looks like the guy in that vision thing we both got, and we can rule out the Extramagus." I caught myself twirling my hair. Thinking about the Extramagus and our wrong-way Luck had me more upset than I wanted to admit.

"No such luck." Blaine ran a hand through his hair and sighed.

"Ten more points to Slytherin if you can tell me why Henry can't give us a description."

"Master-level Mentor Man decided to wipe himself out of bunches of memories and hide for some reason."

"Bingo." Blaine pointed one finger at me, then winked. If I hadn't been sitting, I might have fallen over in a swoon. He was downright sexy when he got studious like that. "Damn, girl. You're going to win the House Cup for Slytherin all by yourself."

I smirked, thinking of at least seven other things I'd rather win than some fictional award from a series of novels about a magical school. Blaine slowly opened his eyes, the smile draining from his face. I watched his Adam's apple bob as he took one step closer to me, but he stopped and turned back to his computer.

"So, how are we going to find out who the black-hat guy is if Henry doesn't know?"

"He's got memories stockpiled somewhere." Blaine rattled a few more messages out on the keyboard. "He's been checking them, but it's a tiring thing. Might take him years."

"We don't have years." I sighed.

"I know." He looked over his shoulder. "We also don't have much help. No one's in town. Henry and Maddie are in Vermont, and they can only take the night bus back, Josh and Nox won't get here until tomorrow, and Bobby and Lynn are in Louisiana. All we have is Tony, and he's hinkier than a hinkfest in Hinktown."

"What about Jeannie?"

"She's not part of the pack." He shook his head. "Knows nothing about the whole Extramagus thing."

"Are you sure?" My question made Blaine freeze.

"She shouldn't." He ran a hand through his hair. Loud music or no, I still couldn't tell him about Ismail, and where I'd found his lamp in the first place.

"She's a Resident Assistant." I shrugged. "The ones at The

Academy seem to know everything all the time about all of us. Shouldn't isn't the same thing as doesn't."

"She did put Nox up in her room during all that Faerie trial business." Smoke trailed out of Blaine's nose. He opened his mouth, and a siren went off.

When he bolted for the door, I followed him. There wasn't any reason to take off after him besides the bracelets, but I did it anyway. Before he ran past me, his face went as white as chalk. Whatever had caused this alarm was beyond serious business.

During the running, I started recognizing my surroundings. We were headed back to the vault, the part of the hoard Blaine had caught me in at the beginning of this whole mess. I almost turned back, feeling like the biggest idiot in the universe for not bringing my bag and Ismail's lamp. I'd come to realize Blaine wanted to help me, but he didn't know how. I had the answer to that in the drawer of the nightstand, but I'd never find my way up there and back in time, even if I didn't get lost on the way. I'd thought maybe it was the perfect situation to get back on track for saving Dad, but I was wrong.

The door was open, sculptures toppled, displays broken, jewelry strewn like bright bits of shattered armor on a silenced battlefield. Blaine didn't stop for that, and neither did I. Instead, I followed in his wake like a small craft trailing an ocean liner on a collision course with an iceberg. We heard the scuff of shoes on marble scant seconds after the scrabble of little claws.

"Friggin' cockatrice again already?" Blaine muttered under his breath. I understood. One of those had almost killed Josh Dennison.

But I didn't smell a cockatrice. I wondered why he didn't realize that, although whatever had gotten in here was small. It smelled like dank, muddy fur and chitin, with no hint of venom. Almost at the back of the vault, a ring of bookcases towered like Stonehenge. They all faced away from us, plain oaken backs giving a starker and more forbidding feel than if they'd been placed with the book side in view. The space they encompassed was large enough to hold a full-grown dragon shifter and a half. Even Blaine hesitated, an homage to the fact that this was a place even he hadn't been, and likely shouldn't go even in an emergency.

A deep growl of frustration came from the other side of stacks weird enough to grace a Scottish heath. That got Blaine moving again. I followed him, dodging around one bookcase and then another until we stood together inside the ring. At the center was an egg the size of a year-old human baby. Its shell was mottled, sky-blue and poison-green. The man on the other side was hardly recognizable as Blaine's stepfather. His clothing was in tatters, and his hair was gone. All his visible skin was covered in skim-milk-white scales with blue edging. I watched him duck and bend, missing something that skittered across the floor.

And that was the source of that smell. *Herpestidae ichneumon*, also known as a Pharaoh's Rat. I'd studied them for a report in my Fall semester, but I'd never seen one. It looked something like a mongoose, but with long fur standing up in muddy spikes. It had quills along its spine, reminding me of a shoddily-armored porcupine. Because I couldn't remember whether they had magic, I checked its energy. It gleamed with pure golden Luck as it faked to one side and another, baiting Mr. Harcourt. Movement by the egg caught my eye. The Pharaoh's Rat Blaine's stepfather faced wasn't alone. A second one was going for the helpless egg, and it had good Luck layered on its energy, too. I felt the air change, going warmer next to me. Blaine was either preparing to flame or shift, actions that could get him or the rest of us killed. Pharaoh's Rats were deadly to dragons, able to burrow in for a long, slow, inevitable kill by internal hemorrhage. I couldn't let that happen to Blaine.

So I pushed him. Blaine toppled directly into one of the bookcases, sending it crashing into the one beside it. He scrambled to stop the avalanche of shelves and tomes and I stepped between the second Pharaoh's Rat and the egg, taking the action Blaine and his stepfather shouldn't. *Herpestidae ichneumon* preyed on full-grown dragons and their eggs, a dragon shifter's only natural predator. They had little to fear, especially since they could make themselves look like a ferret or a weasel even to Psychics and almost every kind of Magus. But Pharaoh's Rats feared Tanuki. We saw through their illusions and were too small for their burrowing tactic to work. We also matched them in speed, but only when shifted.

My skin furred over, the old familiar itch covering every inch of my body. I felt myself change in the shoulders, hips, and hands. Losing my thumbs always sucked. If I'd been a raccoon shifter instead of a canine resembling one, we wouldn't be packing the kind of magic I'd need to defeat this weaselly little rat in time.

I dashed directly toward the Pharaoh's Rat going for the egg. It dodged just a hairsbreadth short of me, and I discovered it was female. One touch would be all I needed to turn her Luck bad. I might even be able to figure out where she and her mate had come from. Pharaoh's Rats weren't shifters, or even sentient. They couldn't manipulate magic. They also couldn't break into locked vaults, so someone must have sent them in here. Whether it was an inside job or magic, I didn't know. The rat tried to get past me again to the egg, and that was when I caught her by the tail.

I stared, watching the gold in her Luck energy tarnish, turning dull and brassy like mine. Bad Luck was contagious, and although she couldn't make hers affect mine, the reverse was not true. My Luck had tap-danced all over hers. She locked gazes with me, then looked over my head, and a trilled call something like a chuckle left her throat. I bit down harder and shook her. The creature's head hit the floor, rendering her an unconscious heap.

I shivered at the displacement in the air and a chilly breeze that couldn't have come from outside. When I turned to leap at the male, it was too late. Mr. Harcourt had fully shifted in order to use the full force of his magical Air breath on the male Pharaoh's Rat. His open mouth made him vulnerable, making me think he was either stupid or so desperate to save his egg that he didn't mind risking death.

I made one last desperate lunge at the creature's hindquarters and tail, but missed. It had gone down poor Wilfred Harcourt's throat.

Only one thing could save him now. I'd have to use one of the Luck charms I'd come here to steal.

CHAPTER THIRTEEN

Blaine

"Dad, no!" My tongue didn't care that Wilfred wasn't my bio-dad. Neither did the rest of me. I dashed across the room, unable to believe what I'd just seen. I could have been a victim, too, if Kimiko hadn't knocked me out of the way. Pharaoh's Rats could burrow into a dragon shifter in human form, though it was harder for them to get in.

My dragonish eyes had let me track her movements, so I knew she'd tried to stop the beast from entering my stepfather's belly. After that, Kimiko took off, a howling brown-beige streak, and I didn't know why. She sounded nothing like a wolf, more like a fox's high-pitched wail. My stepdad shuddered all over, then coughed. Blood dribbled from the corner of his mouth, but no gore stained his teeth. Wilfred hadn't been able to bite down on it in time, then. He flopped on his side and scrabbled at his chest as though something in there hurt him. I knew it did. I gulped.

My legs wouldn't hold me up anymore. I sank to my knees next to the wintry-scaled and twitching form of the guy who'd taught me to knot a tie and fold a pocket handkerchief. Living with Wilfred had been a little like living with a Vulcan most of the time. His lack of demonstrated emotion didn't make me immune to mine. Watching him die felt like watching an old and solid boulder on the cliff walk topple into the bay during a storm surge.

And he *was* dying. The Pharaoh's Rat was in his belly, tearing him up. My teeth gnashed, my fists clenched in my hair, my eyes searched the room as my mind cycled through every item in this vault that might save him. There had to be something, a magic trinket or an ancient device to stop this. I didn't understand why he'd shifted until I really looked at the egg. The pale blue splotches on the shell meant it was his. Wilfred had finally gotten the heir he'd always wanted. And if I failed to think of something, he'd never live to see his whelp hatch.

A flurry of light footsteps and the scent of Chanel Beige brushed past. Mother. Her face held a static expression as she took in the scene as immobile as an ancient Greek theater mask. Except hers wasn't Melpomene's tragedy or Thalia's comedy. Mother's features paused somewhere in between. And that's why I didn't see it coming in time to stop her.

A bright flash of reflected light, a sound like a ruptured tire, a smell like rusted-shut ingots pried open, and the acrid taste of bile in my mouth. Blood like a fountain from Wilfred's throat, Mother's hand embracing the hilt of a stardust-bladed dagger, more tightly than she'd ever clasped his in affection. He stilled immediately, except for the Pharaoh's Rat writhing beneath the thin flesh under his ribs. Mother drew her blood-soaked arm back, plunging the dagger against him one more time. A muffled shriek blossomed, unfolding in pitch and volume as she twisted, killing the rat. And it was over.

Kimiko lowered her head and crept practically on her belly

toward me, dropping a pair of gold cufflinks between us. She quivered against my side, shifting back to her human shape, as shameless of her nudity as Eve that first day in Eden. She clung to me, eyes on Mother, who'd paced over to the egg. With her clean hand, she caressed the shell, humming some lullaby I wasn't sure I could recall. Maybe I didn't want to remember it. No one had ever told me how my father had died. If it'd been like this, I definitely didn't want to find out now.

"He wanted to disinherit you, you know." Mother's voice was husky, low but not sweet. "Cut you off completely once you graduated, and all because of the little one in here. I was having none of that. But he wouldn't agree to an equal split. I found papers. He'd been trying to use his title as leverage with the Flights to get them changed behind my back."

I wanted to ask her so many things. Why the flurry of excuses? All I could think was, had she talked this way about my father when he died?

"Mother, you don't have to—" I couldn't listen to her trash Wilfred like this now.

"Oh, but I do since it should have been me." She turned, her eyes boring into mine but her hand still on the egg. She clenched her free hand, blood dripping from it. "I was supposed to be down here, but he gave me a break so you and I could have our discussion earlier. Otherwise, I'd have gone to my grave thinking it was he who did me in."

"Wait." Kimiko peered around me. "This is going to be a big problem for you, Mrs. Harcourt. You'll be a suspect in his death."

"I know." She turned that Eye of Sauron gaze on Kimiko. I wrapped one arm around her in an instinctive gesture of protection. "You won't, Kimiko." Mother kicked the unconscious Pharaoh's Rat. It was only then that I noticed her feet were bare. "In fact, I'd let you take those Lucky cufflinks you were burgling last night and let you go, but I can't now. At least, not until Blaine does something for me."

I glanced at the girl in my arms as the hope lighting her eyes plunged into a desert island despair. Her silence was an epic to rival *The Odyssey*. She had to save her dad, and I was more determined than ever to help her do it. I stood, scooping up the cufflinks and helping her up along with me. I dropped the Luck charms in the front pocket of my overshirt.

"What's your price, Mother?" I shrugged off my flannel shirt and wrapped it around Kimiko's shoulders. She put her arms in the sleeves.

"Take this thing and examine it for psychic and magical tampering." Mother kicked the weaselly little would-be killer harder, propelling it in my direction. "Go down to Newport PD and tell the police everything you find out about it. After that, she can take her prize wherever it needs to go."

She knew. Mother had known all along what Kimiko had been after, and maybe even why. She'd made an agreement with Mr. Ichiro to betroth us, wiped our memories, and let her future in-law suffer through rapid aging. I couldn't imagine a legitimate reason for even a woman as ruthless and hard-hearted as my mother to do those things.

My teeth squeaked as I ground them together. The smoke I'd been making softened her features and the gory sight of my dead stepfather like a silk filter on a camera from the Golden Age of Hollywood. I picked up the Pharaoh's Rat by its tail and put my other arm around Kimiko's waist.

"When she leaves, I'm going with her and not coming back."

"You can't." Mother's tone brooked no argument, but I wouldn't let her order me around like that. Not after all of this.

"I will." I turned my back on Mother, but Kimiko didn't come along with me like an obedient little Tanuki fiancée. She wasn't one, thank Tiamat.

"You won't leave forever." I glanced back to see my betrothed shaking her head. "I'll send you back, at least for a little while." She reached out and took my hand. "You need to mourn the man who helped kind of raise you. I'll be your plus one if you need that, too."

I almost argued with Kimiko but saw Mother's face blanch. The red of her lipstick stood out even more than the blood that soaked her right hand. She'd stayed composed all through mercy-killing her husband and making her little devil's deal with us. What could have her in a full-on freak-out mode now? I told myself I didn't care.

"Okay. We'll examine this, but I'm not heading to the PD. I'm calling them in. This is an Extrahuman crime scene, and they need to investigate it, not just take a statement from one witness." I held up the deadly rodent and shook it. "After that, we leave. I'll upload my report to the hoard database at my convenience. We'll be back in time for the Mourning Day. Even if Newport's Finest decide to lock you up, I'll be here, keeping up appearances and observing tradition."

This time, when I turned my back and paced away, Kimiko walked beside me.

CHAPTER FOURTEEN

Kimiko

When the detectives showed up, Klein stayed outside with us while Detective Weaver went to question Mrs. Harcourt. Blaine seemed relieved about that. The vampire detective grinned, hiding his fangs as he ran a hand through his mullet to fluff it. I held the cage we had the Pharaoh's Rat in, wearing jeans, a t-shirt, and the flannel I'd worn up to my room from the vault. I had my handbag and Ismail's lamp with me, too. Blaine stood with his back to most of the lawn along the cliff walk. He glared at the creature that had almost killed a whelp in its egg. When Blaine shifted, his eyes went red and slitted first.

"Watching this kind of thing never gets old." Detective Klein jerked his chin at Blaine's clawed feet, his lengthening snout, the wings unfurling like mainsails.

My breath caught in my throat at the sight of his orange scales glittering under the light from the mansion. I was struck by the fact of his physical presence, not in a romantic way.

Looking at Blaine in dragon form was like watching a bonfire or a thunderstorm. He was a thing of natural beauty, powerful and barely constrained. I felt utterly defenseless, faced with the fact that I was expected to marry and produce heirs for two families with a creature like him. I wasn't anywhere near worthy. And then, he was inside my mind.

"Great Egg of Tiamat." The version of his voice in my head was softer than I could have registered it with even my Tanuki ears. "That's how you see me?" He shouldn't have known that.

But he did. Blaine was everywhere in my mind, able to see or hear or sense all my thoughts and feelings. I'd done nothing to shield my psyche, hide my secrets. I closed my eyes and thought of descending curtains, closing doors, the storm barrier shutting during Hurricane Sandy.

"Sorry." I imagined saying the word to him in the interrogation room I'd spent seven hours in the night before Dad decided to send me to The Academy. "Never done this before."

"Huh. Interesting choice. Never been in one of these." I felt his smirk instead of imagining it. "Anyway, this is good. It's a place where Klein can't hear us. Just be careful not to answer stuff I say in here out loud, okay?"

"Wow. Unfair advantage much?"

"There's a reason dragons are almost at the top of the Extrahuman food chain. Open your eyes. Klein's looking at you funny."

"Sorry, Detective." I opened my eyes, giving the vampire the same gracious smile my mom used to give Dad's clients. "Never had the dragon mind-meld before."

"Heavy, huh?" Klein nodded gravely, an ironic contrast with his slang. The moon had set already, a fact that had Klein shifting his weight from one foot to the other and glancing past Blaine's bulk toward the east. "Anyway, let's talk about what we all see here."

"There's something you can find that we won't?" Blaine

snorted along with the snide telepathic question. His "voice" had an echo, like the reverberation on a microphone prone to feedback squeaks. I wasn't sure why but decided it was probably because both the detective and I could hear him.

"Ayup." The detective put his hands in his pockets. "There's a reason Newport PD hired me even after that bastard turned me back in '96. I was top of the heap at State PD as a regular mortal. And there's all the stuff that comes with the vampire senses, too."

"'Kay." Blaine puffed out a smoke ring Gandalf the Gray would have envied. "I'm going to come right out and talk about the elephant in the room. This rat's got some magic on her that shouldn't be there. Faerie. Seelie. Djinn."

I wrapped my arms tightly around my chest, shivering, but not with cold. I took a deep breath, reinforcing my mind's eye view of the interrogation room I'd locked Blaine in. He couldn't know I'd had a Djinn's lamp in my bag all along. I let the breath out. He didn't. Ismail was Unseelie. So, the Extramagus had one of his or her own. I wondered how many wishes they had left.

"You have something to share, Miss Ichiro." Klein's statement came complete with an extra-large helping of suspicion.

"Yeah." I decided to share something besides the ace up my sleeve, though. "It's also got way too much Luck energy on it, still. Like, coincidental levels."

"What do you mean by 'still,' Miss Ichiro?"

"I mean, back in the vault, it had coincidental levels of Luck magic on it, all going deosil in the good Luck direction. I turned its Luck widdershins to defeat it back there like we told you already. But all the Luck should have dissipated by now."

"It smells all wrong." Klein's nostrils flared. "Open the cage."

"No way!" I stepped between him and the Pharaoh's Rat. "If it gets loose, it'll kill him."

"It won't." Klein bared his fangs. "It can't, not anymore."

"Do as he says." The Blaine inside the interrogation room

nodded, grinning and relaxed. The big dragon in front of me played at twitching his wings nervously.

"Then *you* open it." I stepped aside, deciding I wouldn't take orders from either of them. Klein was only slightly less infuriating than Blaine, mostly because I wouldn't have to deal with him for much longer.

The latch made a tiny squeak. When Klein moved his hand away, the creature looked up at him by rolling its eyes. It toppled to one side, wriggling the spikes on its back weakly. I watched its Luck energy swirl faster, like the sparse suds of tepid bathwater spiraling down a drain.

"It's poisoned." Klein tapped his ear. "I can hear its blood getting silty."

"Mother." The Blaine in my head paced along the two-way mirror, seething with anger. On the glass beside him, the image of Hertha Harcourt caressing the egg played like a movie. "She could have scratched it when she kicked it."

"I get it." I imagined myself leaning my elbows on the table in the middle of the room. "She's a poison dragon, so that plus the Seelie energy makes you think she really did mean to kill your stepfather. Don't say anything to Klein yet, though. I have another theory."

"Hold on. All this might add up to something." I pulled my phone from my handbag, tapped it, and opened LORA. I added "poison," "Pharaoh's Rat," and its taxonomic name, *"Herpestidae ichneumon"* to the existing data and parameters. Then I chuckled, which sounded like rain hitting a headstone. I zoomed in on the items it'd be safe to let Klein see, locked the screen, and held the phone out to him. "Check it out."

"This isn't the software we use." Klein tapped the tip of one of his fangs with his tongue. "Huh. Trolls found a whole nest of these critters poisoned under the Pell Bridge last year, Tiverton side."

"And check out the registered Precog prediction." I pointed. "Show it to Blaine, too."

Klein's eyes went wide. He shook his head, turned the phone around. Blaine peered at it, lashing his tail.

"Who's Joyce?" Blaine's voice reverberated.

"Joyce Watkins." Klein sighed. "She died during the Reveal. Her husband disappeared, and no one knows why.

"There's a Professor Watkins at my school," Blaine commented.

"Yeah, Joyce's brother-in-law." He shrugged. "For whatever reason, the husband's full name is escaping me."

"It can only be Edgar." I kept that back from Klein, telling it to the Blaine in the interrogation room. "Your mom and the Headmistress were talking about needing him, remember?"

"Tiamat's Scales!" The words filled the little room. So did more of Blaine's ideas, half-formed and nonverbal alike. His excitement felt like static electricity crackling through the air.

I couldn't handle it. The flood of thoughts and feelings coming from him stormed my lame attempt at a mental fortress like a breaker might topple a sandcastle. I put my hands over my face, then pulled them away wet. I looked down to find tears and blood. Blaine withdrew from my mind, leaving behind a balm of regret and apology.

"Jeez, not blood. Not after the night I've had." Klein's hands shook. He took two steps backward, dropping my phone on the lawn. Then he took another step back toward me. He closed his eyes. "No."

"Good evening, Detective Klein. Miss Ichiro. Young Master Harcourt." A man with terra-cotta-tone skin, jet hair streaked with silver, and nearly black eyes stepped between the hungry vampire and me. "I am Taki Waban, a friend of the family. Forgive the intrusion. We're looking for Mistress Harcourt." One corner of his mouth turned up, and he glanced to his right.

"Hi, I'm Tony." I hadn't noticed the other guy at first. He held out his arm, and I was about to shake his hand until I realized he was handing me a handkerchief. Try saying that five times fast.

"Thanks," I managed. I dabbed my nose and pinched it to stop the bleeding. Klein got a grip on himself and pulled a bag of blood from inside his vest.

"Mother's inside, being questioned by Detective Weaver, sir." This time, there wasn't any reverb when Blaine communicated to us. "You're welcome to wait inside. Gomer will direct you to whatever room she's designated."

"That's just the thing, Young Master." Mr. Waban shook his head. "Gomer is nowhere to be found. I had my suspicions, but..."

"I should have turned that Brownie into a torch when I had the chance."

"You mean the Brownie in my debt since the night Professor Brodsky was apprehended? The one I sent to keep an eye on the two of you?"

Blaine blinked. Tony gasped. I chuckled. Detective Klein scowled.

"It makes sense." I grinned at Mr. Waban. "Gomer's a Seelie Goblin. They're so unusual, the Queen wouldn't want them in her inner circle. No wonder he's a servant in a dragon shifter's house."

"So you think Gomer's been passing information to some flagrantly idiotic person who thinks it's a good idea to mess with the Harcourts?" Tony directed the question at me but pointed his crossed fingers at Blaine from behind his back.

"Yeah." I picked up a lock of my hair, twirling it. "There had to be an informant. It explains the timing of both attacks. The shooters knew exactly where we'd be walking. But they didn't know we'd have a bear shifter to help us. And they expected Mrs. Harcourt to be guarding the egg instead of her husband. Wilfred filled in for her at the last minute."

"I see." Detective Klein wiped his mouth, then gestured at me with the bag of blood. "So, Wilfred Harcourt wasn't a target, but collateral damage. It was Hertha, Blaine, and the egg they wanted. But why bother poisoning the Pharaoh's Rat?"

"Because that way, it'd look like Hertha was trying to bump off someone in the Harcourt family and it went wrong." I told Detective Klein all about Wilfred's attempt to change Blaine's inheritance. Blaine agreed that was the kind of thing his mother might mention to Gomer. "Big tragic mistake. Whoever did this has a mind like a million steel traps."

"And you're at PPC for Extrahuman Crime Investigation, Miss Ichiro?" Klein put his hands on his hips.

"Um, no." I felt my face flush, embarrassed about my actual academic circumstances.

"You should be." Klein tapped my phone and handed it back to me. "And where did you get this app? It's gorgeous."

"She programmed it." Blaine's telepathic words came with three smoke rings. The reverb was back. A nervously pacing human form Blaine appeared along with the interrogation room in my mind's eye. "Your interpretation is nice and all, but it's not the only one. I have a bad feeling about how Weaver might have taken everything, plus the fact that Mother wanted me to go to the PD initially. Do you trust me?" I nodded out on the lawn to him and everyone else. "Good. Stay close and try not to freak out."

"Woah, cool." Klein's smile was like the flash on a camera, blinding and then gone an instant later. "Detective Weaver, hi."

I'd heard footsteps but had been too distracted to check whose they were. But Blaine had known, of course. The spider shifter Detective stepped right up to Blaine's snout, somehow looking down her nose at him even though he was enormous. She flashed her badge.

"Stop getting all buddy-buddy with the dragon, Cal." She narrowed her eyes.

"Wait, what?" Klein blinked at his partner. "I don't get it."

"The house is full of Hertha Harcourt's poison apples. This whelp's never been close to his stepfather, even though he married the mother before Blaine hatched. A sibling means he'll have to split everything if not lose it all. And, according to a note from the Goblin butler, he has connections to the Gitanos and has been entertaining this Tanuki. She's got a record of Grand Theft, you know.

"Blaine Harcourt, you're under arrest for the murder of Wilfred Harcourt, and the attempted murder of your younger sibling. You'll shift back down to human form now and come along peacefully."

But he did no such thing.

CHAPTER FIFTEEN

Blaine

I scooped Kimiko up in my left talon and took off. I didn't worry about Weaver or Klein shooting at us, because the backdraft from my wings knocked them both flat, Taki Waban, too. What I could hardly believe was that Tony Gitano was the last man standing down there. He pumped his fist in the air twice. Before I got out of telepathy range with him, he promised to clear things up. I had my doubts about his ability to do that until I remembered him on the Vespa after the shooting.

He knew things I didn't, especially about any fake Gitano Gang contacts Gomer could have cooked up. I let my wings continue the ascent. Once I was at apex over the Pell Bridge, I'd tilt them and head back down to land at India Point Park, where I had some clothes stashed.

"Blaine?" Kimiko's thoughts gave me double vision, pulling part of my focus back to the interrogation room her imagination had cooked up. "Blaine, why are you running from the police?"

"Because we have to get the Lucky cufflinks to your dad. It sounded like they wanted to bring you in for questioning, too. If I let Weaver and company hold us, he could die before we get out."

She didn't give me anything like a verbal answer. Instead, the drab cinderblock walls in that little made-up room melted away. I was with her in a woodland clearing, sunlit with early morning light. The trees had blossoms, pink and white. The grass was still short and speckled with star-shaped white flowers. A brass lamp sat on a tree stump in the middle, but I didn't care enough about it to examine it more closely. Her arms went around my neck, her body pressed against mine. The warmth of her embrace in my mind was nothing like the mocking playfulness she'd shown when we almost got caught listening in. It was leaps and bounds beyond the brief lip-lock that had spurred the hidden betrothal memories.

Kimiko wasn't just showing me a telepathic display of affection. She was giving me her trust. This sanctuary of her heart and mind opened to my presence, welcoming me in a way I never thought another person would. I'd always been kept at arm's length before.

I lowered some of my own barriers, giving as good as I got. Tiger-lilies sprang up at the tree line, orange like my scales. Fluffy little clouds made dragon shapes in the previously clear sky. The trees sprouted leaves and fruit alongside the blossoms. Our imagination collaboration amalgamated spring and summer, dawn and midday. I wondered whether we'd break into a musical number.

The clearing filled with her laughter, my eyes filled with tears. This place was perfect. She was perfect. Mother had gone and betrothed me to my destined mate after insisting my entire life that I'd be married to make an alliance and would have to pass on anything coincidence might present.

Whether this was some kind of colossal mistake on her part, the Ichiro family Luck, or deliberate misleading from the Precog who'd been standing with the man in the Greek fisherman's hat, I had no idea. All I knew was, Kimiko Ichiro was my destiny, and not some ill fate like I'd imagined earlier that same day. I'd do anything for her now.

"Back at you." Her words were everywhere, not just in my ears. It's hard to explain, but telepathy is like that. It's not just communicating but communion. Her words sang in the breeze, rustled in the branches. They were close enough to be mine, my feelings also hers, our actions like a mirror without glass between the images. I would have kissed her, worried it'd be weird to have our first real one be imaginary.

But just because it was happening in my head didn't make it unreal. We were in both our heads at the same time after all. And neither of us had any idea when we'd get a solid-state chance. What we were doing in the shared mind space was more intimate than kissing, or anything either of us had done with other people. Uncharted territory.

And that's why I didn't think to question the dimming of the sky, the fading of the colors, and the floral scent vanishing. I expected the world to go away, just not for the reason it did.

Kimiko

Letting Blaine into the sanctuary I'd made when my mom died had been a leap of faith to meet his heroic one. He had taken off, defying his mother and the police because he knew my father was almost out of time. If we hadn't already been betrothed, I would have asked Dad to consider him as a marriage prospect. I didn't care that he'd have a record for evading arrest. Neither would the rest of my family, all things considered.

I thought he'd faded away to concentrate on landing. Then I

realized he couldn't be. We weren't anywhere near land, and I'd have sensed that in his thoughts and feelings. The meeting of our minds didn't reveal everything about him, but I'd sensed the part of him focused on flying us to India Point Park. When he faded, nothing indicated a change in course.

At first, I thought he was dropping me, but Blaine's talon had actually gotten smaller. We were close to a thousand feet above Newport Bay, the lights on the Pell Bridge gleaming below against waters too calm for March. His wings merged back into his body, and we fell. His eyes stayed shut. The telepathic link had faded with his consciousness. The miasma of bad Luck around him was almost as thick as what had surrounded that Pharaoh's Rat in the cage just before it died.

I could twist into a dive, but Blaine couldn't. I had just seconds to act before he hit the water with his neck and broke it. Instead of adjusting my fall, I stuck my hand in my bag and rubbed. Ismail appeared, tethered to the lamp inside my handbag. No matter what happened, he'd be okay, could get back into his lamp before impact. He looked from me to Blaine, then back.

"What do you wish?" Ismail's magic made his voice audible even through the rush of free fall. He sounded more dejected than he should have, considering this would be my third and final wish.

"Send us to my Dad immediately."

"No." But Djinn weren't supposed to say that. They were supposed to grant any wish. The Seelie ones did it literally, which is where stories like The Monkey's Paw came from.

"Why?" I had to know, especially since time was running out to make another wish.

"You'll die and take everyone at his house with you." Ismail sighed. I couldn't believe a Djinn could be this helpful without consequences. Him giving me this information was bound to get him in deep trouble. "I can only Vanish you there, but that won't change your movement speed. I'm limited in what I can do, remember?"

"Fine." I made a choice, hoping it was the right one. "I wish our impact and time in the water will leave us both unharmed."

"Done."

The syllable ended, and the thick Luck energy around Blaine brightened until I thought the three of us must look like a falling star. It expanded, encompassing Blaine, Ismail, and me in a bubble. The rushing air stopped whipping my hair into snarls, and it felt like we were floating instead of falling. I reached out to Blaine, holding him close. We hit the water near the Tiverton side at the north of the bridge, where my brother had almost died in a car accident a few years earlier. Actually, we didn't hit the water. It was more like flopping on a memory-foam mattress after a long day.

The bubble dissipated slowly, taking on water like a leaky canoe. We were still in the water though Ismail was gone. He'd be back in his lamp, of course. I reached into my bag, intending to hand it to Blaine so he could use the wishes to get us to Dad. But the lamp was gone, and he was still unconscious. I clung to him, trying to figure out why he wouldn't wake up, even with cold seawater seeping in around us. And then I noticed my wrist.

My tithing bracelet was gone, but Blaine still had his. Only a high-ranking member of the Sidhe Queen's or Goblin King's Court could have removed it. Only one type of Faerie had the power to do something like that from a distance—another Djinn. So, the Extramagus had been out-wishing us, as I suspected. And here I was, stuck with the consequences of having used my last wish to land us in the drink. Why hadn't I wished us into a boat? Of course. My thinking was better done with coding and logic puzzles than on my feet, or in the air, as it turned out. And now, we'd be stuck with the *Titanic* ending instead of the *Pretty Woman* one. I got on my back, holding Blaine's head above water as best as I could, otter-style. Ren might have been proud.

"Come with me if you want to live!" And there was a woman in an actual canoe that wasn't leaky at all holding out an oar.

"Can't, he's TKO!" I hollered back to the woman, who pulled the paddle back into the boat with her. Then she reached down and grabbed Blaine's arms. She hauled him up over the side, biceps and shoulder muscles bulging. That girl had some big guns!

I had to blink when she grabbed me. I thought I saw a shaggy red mane of hair, pointy ears, pallid skin, and clawed nails at the ends of her fingers. A crane couldn't have pulled me from the bay any more effortlessly. She tossed blankets at me. By the time I finished wrapping Blaine up in one of them, I figured it out. Her glamour had slipped. Our rescuer was a Faerie. The boat was heading back to the bridge, not to pass south, but under and perpendicular. We docked in the lee of the bridge on the Tiverton side.

"So you're a Troll."

"And you've got a brain on you. Good." She tied a rope to a cleat on the dock. "You look familiar."

"A few years back, my brother went missing after a car accident here."

"Oh, yeah, I read about the guy who came back from the dead as a Selkie. So you're his Tanuki sister, then."

"And you saved our lives." I smiled. "Thank you."

"Maybe. Don't thank me yet." She had her fingers pressed to Blaine's throat. "His pulse is weak. We have to get him inside." She hoisted him over her shoulder, then got out onto the dock. "Come on."

I followed the Troll until she got to a blank stone wall. She knocked on it, and a hidden door opened, the light a warm red and smoky. Inside was a cave, the ceiling high near the entrance but sloping almost too low for me at the back. A few cots, camp chairs, crates, and an old wood stove furnished the place. The walls were painted in intricate vine designs. A pile of blankets moved on the cot in one corner, and a guy who resembled our rescuer got up, leaving another, smaller bundle behind. He was the same height as her, but stockier and much older.

"Grandpa, this guy has something wrong with him, and it's only getting worse."

"Tithing bracelet. Shouldn't touch it. This is the Harcourt whelp. His mother won't be happy to hear he's with an Unseelie courtier like me. She's a friend of the Queen."

"But she'll be unhappier if he's in a coma." I stepped closer to the big fellow. "If you don't take it off, what'll happen?"

"Depends." Grandpa grunted. "These old Tithing Bracelets knock the wearers out if they get too far from each other. But there's a terminal range. Looks like your friend here ran too far." He turned his back, heading for the cot again.

"But he didn't." I circled, trying to get in front of him again. "The other bracelet was on me, and then it wasn't."

"Huh." He squinted at me, then at Blaine. "Gemma, get my spectacles."

Instead of a pair of glasses, she brought him a contraption that looked more like the lens testers at an Optometrist's office. He strapped it on his head and lowered one huge lens over his right eye and a tiny one over his left. Then, he peered at us again.

"You're telling me the truth. But what in the name of the King did you do to anger a Seelie Djinn?"

"Saved a life." I gazed down at Blaine. "And he saved a soul." I reached out and brushed a wet lock of hair off his cheek. A faint golden glow swirled over my hand. Luck. And it was turning in the right direction, finally. But Blaine had none around him at all. "And your question's a test because Djinn can't do anything like wishing a Tithing Bracelet off one person and on to another unless they're doing time in a lamp."

"See, Grandpa?" Gemma held Blaine's arm up. "I fished up a couple of heroes. Now, why don't you help them already?"

"Heroes?" Grandpa chuckled. "Hardly. Well, I always wanted

to have a favor owed from Hertha Harcourt." But when he tried to unclasp the Tithing Bracelet, it wouldn't budge. "Now that's curious. Most curious indeed." He flipped down a few more lenses on his spectacle contraption. "It seems I'm not high-ranked enough to take this bracelet off."

"What?" I trembled, a sinking sensation starting in my gut that was even worse than the free-fall earlier.

"I'm an Admiral, equal to a Marquess, and it's still not good enough. You'll need someone else."

"But he's dying."

"I know." Grandpa shuffled across to the corner opposite from where he'd been sleeping. "Here." He threw a sack at Gemma. "Have it Vanish them to the Duke's house immediately."

I peered at the sack as it squirmed. What did he have in there, a kitten? But when Gemma opened it, a little creature with a pointy hat stuck its head out. A Gnome. She brought it over, muttering something in what sounded like a Middle Eastern tongue. It took one look at Blaine and then haggled with her. She rolled her eyes.

"It won't Vanish them unless we free it from all further oblig-ation, Grandpa."

"Fine, whatever. Make the deal." Grandpa waved his hand. "It's worth losing a Gnome's favor in order to get one from the Harcourts."

I assume Gemma's next words were an agreement to the Gnome's terms. An instant later, I felt the weird sensation of disintegration as I vanished from the Tiverton Troll cave. When I properly had eyes again, I found myself on a meticulously crafted porch. Blaine was in front of me, laying on the planks. I sat, drawing his head into my lap in hopes that he'd be more comfortable. The mailbox had the name Redford engraved on it. Gemma stood at the front door to the most well-constructed house I'd ever laid eyes on. She rang the bell.

"Uh, hi?" The guy who answered the door looked familiar

from when I'd cased the PPC campus. He wore a red Paw Sox cap and a t-shirt with the Coca-Cola logo on it.

"Fred, get your dad. This is some serious Unseelie business."

"Great Goblin's Garters, is that Blaine Harcourt?"

"Yes." I'd heard of Fred Redford being a stand-up guy, also friends with Josh Dennison. "He needs this Tithing Bracelet off ten minutes ago."

Fred didn't say a word, just took off running into the house. He was back in moments with his dad. Neil Redford looked like a regular guy until he hunkered down next to Blaine. After that, he let his glamour down. Tithed Faerie courtiers could control that kind of thing in a way their Changeling offspring couldn't. I glanced at Fred. His glamour slipped, revealing the same grayish skin, pointy teeth, and red eyes as his father's. Gemma's held for the most part, although her hair got wilder looking for a second or two.

"What happened?" Blaine rubbed his hands over his face. While I'd been distracted by the glamour, Duke Neil Redford had taken the life-threatening jewelry off.

"Not much." I reached for Blaine but hesitated. He met me halfway, taking my hand in both of his. "Fell out of the sky, got rescued by Gemma the Troll from Tiverton, a Gnome Vanished us to Providence, and then Duke Redford here got rid of your Tithing Bracelet."

"How in Tiamat's name did we survive all that?" His eyes went wide. "You didn't burn the Luck charm—"

"No." I sighed. "That's a long story for another time. I have to get to Dad's."

"Okay, I'll drive you over." Fred jingled some keys in his pocket.

"I'll call Lyft for Gemma." Mr. Redford pulled a phone from his pocket. "Tell your grandfather our debt is settled now."

Fred and I helped Blaine into an extended-cab pickup truck. I held my betrothed's hand the whole way home.

CHAPTER SIXTEEN

Blaine

Fred's truck rattled over pavement sorely in need of repair. At least that was what it felt like for my poor head. Kimiko and Fred both seemed immune to all the jostling. My wrist tingled, fingers numb but coming back to life. How had the tithing bracelet become a danger when Kimiko and I were touching? It made about as much sense as anything else over the last twenty-four hours, which was absolutely none at all. There was one time I'd been close to figuring it all out. The mental merge with Kimiko had given me new inspiration, bigger insight. If only I could get some of that mojo back, but I was too weak to shift even partially.

"Long story or not, can you give me an elevator pitch?" I kept the request to a murmur. "Fred knows what's in the files I gave you."

"Yeah, I'd like to know what's going on, too." I'd forgotten about Fred's big, pointy Redcap ears.

"Fine." Kimiko tapped her fingers against the window. "All the trouble since I got to Newport came from Djinns. I had no idea that using wishes would let an Extramagus counter me with them, too."

"Of course not. You didn't even know there was an Extramagus until after the Gitanos shot at us."

"What!" Fred's shout went through my head like an ice pick. "Tony would never do something like that."

"And he didn't. He warned us, actually." Kimiko picked up my still numb hand and rubbed it. It was almost like she knew it bothered me. Her touch brought some warmth and sensation back, but it ached. "Anyway, we were flying along perfectly fine when you just passed out. I wished us a safe landing. It was my third wish, too, so the idea was to hand you the lamp. But even if you hadn't been unconscious, it was gone."

"So you think the Extramagus wished for your bracelet to move over to someone else?"

"Wow, that means his Djinn is a Duke or better. You can't just wish a Tithing Bracelet off with a low-ranking one." Fred turned left on Angell Street. "They get extra powers from whatever else used to be in the lamp, but Djinn still have limits."

"Yeah. I've got the feeling my Djinn was pretty low on the totem pole. He was Unseelie but still bent the rules way more than I expected. Gave me advice and stuff. Well, at least we don't have to worry about the Extramagus making any more wishes since we already got attacked three times."

"You know, I'm not sure all three of his wishes got used."

"No? Why?"

"Because the Gatto shooting and the Pharaoh's Rat attack might not have come from the Extramagus." I sighed. "The Gatto Gang hates your dad, remember? Plus, there's too much bad blood and paranoia between Mother's generation of dragon shifters. Our investigation only made things more confusing."

"Not really." Kimiko brought out her phone, but it wouldn't

turn on, let alone open the LORA app again. "I didn't show Detective Klein the whole picture. But I'm still missing a piece. What did you realize before you got out of my head back on your lawn?"

"Okay, so there had to be something besides the guy who wiped our memories at our betrothal ceremony."

The truck's wheels screeched as Fred slammed on the brakes. He swerved, pulling over in front of a hydrant across the street from the Ichiro house. His arm moved jerkily, slamming the transmission into Park. Then, the Redcap unbuckled his seatbelt and turned to stare into the extended cab at us.

"Great Goblin's Garters!" He shook his head, Paw Sox cap bobbing. "You're betrothed? You two? That's insane! No one ever tells me anything."

"We only just found out ourselves tonight, okay? Chill out, man." I glanced at Kimiko. She rolled her eyes, of course. I rolled mine back, and she giggled. "You're perfect. You know that, right?"

Her jaw went slack, and she blinked. The rear door opened, and a chilly gust blew in with Fred's fake gagging noises.

"Okay, you two. Get out. You don't have to go home, but you can't stay here."

"Um, actually Fred, we do have to go home." Kimiko jerked her chin at the little white house on the other side of the street. "I kinda sorta live there, you know." She clutched her handbag tightly to her chest, looked both ways, and crossed the street.

I followed, steadier on my feet than I'd been getting into the truck. Fred pulled away, honking as he left. A light went on inside, and by the time I got to the bottom step, the front door opened.

"Kim?" Ren Ichiro stood in the doorway, eyes on his sister. He glanced at me, then did a double-take. "Harcourt. You'd better not be the reason she's been missing."

"Nope, not me. My mother."

"There's no time for this." Kim put her hands on her hips. "I need to see Dad."

"Fine. Go in and see him, but he's in a bad way." Ren stepped aside and she went down the hall, then up the stairs. I went after her, but her brother stopped me. "No. He's dying, you know. She should say goodbye to him alone. Sit in the kitchen with the others. That's the door to the right of the stairs."

Before I could ask what he meant by saying goodbye and others, Ren shut the front door and headed left into a darkened parlor. I didn't want to mess with an angry Selkie, so I turned right at the bottom of the stairs. Josh Dennison was standing in the middle of the modest kitchen with his hand stretched out toward his sister Beth. She faced what had to be the back door, one hand resting lightly on the doorknob. Josh's mate, Nox Phillips, sat on a stool at the kitchen counter, one hand pressed over her eyes.

"What did I just walk in on here?" I glanced from Josh to Beth. Neither of them looked at me.

"Impending wolfy challenge." At least Nox was in a talking mood.

"I'm too tired for this." I shuffled to the stool next to hers and sat. "Just. Too. Tired."

"Wait, why?" Something in my voice must have snapped Josh out of whatever wolfy angst state he'd been in. Or maybe there was some Alpha wolf wooj going on.

"Oh, the usual stuff for us mad Tinfoil Hatters." I didn't shrug, just stared at Josh. "Using my wings as a kevlar shield, watching Mother mercy-kill Wilfred, running from the detective trying to arrest me, the thousand-foot free-fall next to the Pell Bridge, Tithing Bracelets gone wild."

Nox gasped. Beth dropped her hand from the doorknob.

"Leaping Luna!" Josh took three steps back toward the counter and leaned, looking me in the eye. "Wilfred's dead? Your stepdad? How?"

"And kevlar? Did someone shoot at you?" Nox tugged my sleeve.

I didn't turn to look at her, wanted just to forget she and Beth were even in the room. This was all on Josh. Kimiko and I wouldn't have been in this kind of trouble if we hadn't helped him. Besides, even if I didn't feel like it was all his fault, Josh Dennison was the leader of my pack. Any Extrahuman would hold him accountable for my safety, even if that wouldn't hold up in a court of law.

"It's only been hours since we talked on the phone, but this is a long story." I didn't remember or care whether Beth knew about the Extramagus or not. Most of what I had to say would be all over the papers and the news apps in the morning, anyway. "You might not believe it all, and I don't blame you. I wouldn't if it hadn't happened to me."

I told him all of it, not stopping when Ren quietly entered the room and took a seat at the breakfast table. Despite my disclaimer, all four of them believed me.

CHAPTER SEVENTEEN

Kimiko

I didn't skip the seventh step or the thirteenth. Refusing to sneak upstairs felt like I'd defied myself for once instead of Dad. After all the rebellion and sass in the decade since Mom died and the fact that I might still be too late, letting the creaky stairs announce my presence could be the most adult thing I'd ever done.

Dad had lived in the room at the end of the hall since Mom died. Why was it always this way, a long walk and too much time to think when we didn't want it but not enough when we did? This collection of moments stretched out, bits and bobs of time I'd have preferred metered out during the free-fall above the Bay. But we have to take time however we get it. The universe gives us no other choice.

The fact that Blaine felt his own guilt over Wilfred almost as strongly as I felt mine over Dad might have been comforting to regular humans. For Extrahumans, parallels like this smacked of coincidence. He had still been in the egg when Blaine lost the man who had sired him, and he'd lost the next best thing tonight. I'd lost my mom ten years ago. Coincidence seemed to indicate that my dad would die this evening too.

The door was ajar. I pushed by just enough to pass, not wanting to risk disturbing anything that belonged to my family more than I already had. I wouldn't have needed my enhanced hearing to listen to the sound of Dad's breathing. The breaths were shallow, uneven, the spaces between them more terrifying than that free-fall over the Bay. And I wondered how much of the two centuries he'd been alive had tallied their marks on his face, his body, his health. But I cut the speculation and stepped to his bedside. I had no excuse but cowardice to wonder when I could see for myself.

And it didn't look as bad as I'd imagined. His face mapped out more lines than I'd seen framing Taki Waban's eyes and hairline, but not as many as Professor Nate Watkins. And his color was higher than Henrietta Thurston's. My mouth dropped open. I squinted, trying to detect magic. I couldn't, of course. All a Tanuki like me could see was Luck, and that was there, just barely a glimmer. I closed my eyes, wishing Ismail could still help me, or that the telepathic bond between Blaine and me hadn't been severed. Then I realized that someone could tell me what had happened. Dad. But first, he needed my help.

I'd stowed the cufflinks in the front pocket of my jeans when I'd changed, in case Hertha Harcourt changed her mind about letting me have them. Good call, considering my dip in the Bay had washed out half the contents of my handbag. The room brightened as I pulled them out and opened my fist, as though the Luck in them knew where it had to go.

Dad's hand felt like an old book, leathery and heavy. When I tipped the cufflinks into the cup of his palm and closed his fingers over them, the surrounding glow dimmed, but his eyes opened. Rheumy brown irises gave way to gold. Dry lips parted as he mouthed my name. His breath went in and out like the bellows he used to get the fireplace going in winter.

"Kimi, get the lights." His voice wasn't up to closing arguments volume, but it was close enough. I just barely made out his hand going to the front pocket of his pajama shirt, but my ears picked up the muffled clink of the cufflinks dropping in.

"Anything, Daddy." My eyes stung as I fumbled blindly at the panel. I'd gone through all that—wishing myself into a hoard, defying scary old dragons, being shot at, fighting Pharaoh's Rats and getting dropped from a thousand feet—and now here I was, unable to flip a light switch. Finally, I made contact, but by then, I was crying. The last thing I wanted to do was let Dad see that.

I leaned my forehead against the wall, mouth open and eyes shut, forehead pressed against cool plaster and a hot flood on my cheeks. I put a silencer on my vocal cords, but the rush of my breathing, intermittent like Morse Code, whooshed in my ears, drowning all other sounds. All the same, the renewed Luck energy around my father told me he'd gotten up and come to comfort me. His hand on my shoulder reminded me of the last time we'd been together this way, the night Mom died. I opened my eyes.

"I always knew you'd do it." The rubber tipped end of a cane dented the carpet to the left of his feet. I swallowed past the bottled up angst I'd been carrying since I realized Dad was aging without his pin.

"Do what?" I couldn't look at him yet, not anything but his feet, anyway.

"Come through this. Be a hero." He patted my shoulder. "Make me proud."

"But I almost killed you."

"I knew you wouldn't." He didn't lead me to any conclusions.

But he never did. He always expected me to figure things out on my own.

"Joyce Watkins. The Precognitive."

"Yes. She was the best in Rhode Island. And one of her last predictions had to do with you and Blaine Harcourt."

"Our betrothal?"

"No. She fibbed on that one, said the two of you weren't destined. Otherwise, Hertha would never have agreed to the arrangement."

"Why?"

"She believes her son should be spared any chance of heartbreak."

"That's twisted. I mean, what if he met his mate after he'd gone and married someone else?"

"He'd be expected to ignore her, the same way she ignored coincidence's choice for her to marry Wilfred instead. Your future mother-in-law hasn't got a heart of stone, but she's encased it in ice nearly her whole life."

"How did you manage to stay alive? You look in better shape than I expected."

"I got help. Some old friends helped slow down my aging." He sighed. "I have more work to do."

"Brodsky's trial." Blaine was the only other person who could make me look away from my father at that moment. "You're defending him."

"Perhaps. But you don't work for me." Dad's chuckle turned into a cough. "Even if I didn't need rest, I can't discuss my clients or cases with anyone but my staff."

"I get it." Blaine put his arm around me. "You need sleep. And so does Kimiko if she's going to hold me to that promise I made back when we left the vault."

"Go. You're welcome to rest in my house." Dad limped back to his bed and got in it, then closed his eyes. His breathing sounded normal now.

"Come on." I took Blaine's hand and led him out of the room, closing the door behind me. We stopped at a room across from mine. When I opened the door, Blaine hesitated.

"A guest room? Really?" He blinked, eyes round. "After all we've been through?"

"Dad wouldn't mind, but Ren wasn't so happy to see you."

"That was before the discussion we had with Josh, Nox, and Beth in the kitchen." He sighed, shifting his weight from one foot to the other. Somehow he managed to look exhausted and nervous at the same time. "Actually, it was more like the Harcourt Family Roast. But anyway, Ren understands now. I couldn't believe it, but he said he thinks the betrothal's a good thing." He closed the door to the guest room and crossed the hall in one giant step.

"I'm a complete mess."

"So am I, in more ways than one."

"I'm exhausted and tomorrow will be a long day regardless of whether we get thrown in the Newport jail or go to a dragon funeral."

"Same here." He leaned against the wall as I stood in the doorway. "But I don't want to be alone."

"Neither do I." I stepped backward, letting him in.

Blaine headed for my desk, but I waved him at the bed and told him to rest. I needed to get Eau de Bay out of my hair, so I grabbed a towel and pajamas and went down the hall to the bathroom. On the way back, I grabbed a towel for him from the linen closet. A red backpack sat outside the door, so I brought that in with me, too.

"So, someone left this. Maybe it made an ass out of you and me, but I just assumed it's yours."

"It is. Josh brought it over from India Point Park." He got up from the bed, stretching.

"Isn't that where we were headed before?"

"Yeah. It's one of the few places in town where my dragon fits." Blaine stepped up to stand in the doorway.

"So he went all the way over there just to get you a change of clothes?"

"Yeah." His cheeks reddened as he reached for the bag. "I used to think they all just kind of tolerated me, you know?"

"I understand." I let my hand linger on his for a moment, and he rewarded me with a smile. "Tagging you in for the bathroom match."

"Awesomesauce."

I curled up on my bed with my dank handbag on top of the nightstand and my completely ruined phone in my hands. It wouldn't turn on, waterlogged as it was. All the data on LORA might as well have been on Pluto. I'd downloaded everything to the tablets in Blaine's room, but wouldn't be able to get them unless Detectives Klein and Weaver weren't waiting to snag us the second we set foot in their jurisdiction. Something occurred to me just as Blaine came back in, hair still damp from the shower.

"Why would Weaver try to arrest you when she had exactly the same story Klein did?"

"Woah, you don't waste any time." He lifted the towel off his shoulders and rubbed his hair with it. "Hmm. A gorgeous woman once told me how Occam had a Razor, and he knew how to use it. I'd say she didn't get the same story we gave Klein."

"But we told him the truth." I dropped my useless phone back in my handbag. It made a squishy sound.

"I know, which means Mother didn't." He rattled off a few words in a language I didn't recognize. Probably a list of things people who had normal mothers wouldn't call them.

"Look, there has to be a reason." I stood and held a hand out to him. "Maybe Weaver's hinky, connected to the Extramagus somehow?"

"Simplest is, Mother told a lie. It's what she does." He took my hand, using it to draw me closer. "And there doesn't always have to be a reason for her to do it."

"Well, either way, is it going to stop you from trying to attend your stepdad's Mourning Day?"

"No." Blaine put his arms around me. "That same gorgeous woman said I need to mourn him, and she was right. Also, just about everyone's coming with me."

"Everyone?"

"Yeah, all of Tinfoil Hat. Josh, Nox, Ren. Bobby and Lynn are flying up early. Tony the hinky cat. Fred. Olivia. Jeannie. Even Henry and Maddie will show up after sundown, despite the fact that they can't actually come into the house because of the egg." He walked me over to the bed and sat on the edge of it with me. "The people in that pack of misfit toys I hang around with are the real deal. I started talking, and Josh got everyone who was out of town on speakerphone. I told them everything, not just what happened in the vault with Wilfred dying. All of it. About Mother and the paranoia all those years. And once I was done talking, I saw their faces. Knew for sure nothing about my life growing up was normal. And you know what?"

"What?" I put my legs in his lap and leaned against his chest.

"The thing that scared me most about finding that out didn't happen. They believed me like real friends are supposed to, even when the basics of my life seemed impossible to them. And that is why they'll all be there tomorrow. Even if we're in a holding cell or something, people will still be there for Wilfred. And me."

There was nothing to say to that. Instead, I let him hold me close and hugged him back. Blaine's mom had said some choice words about Wilfred, but that didn't stop Blaine from caring that he'd died. And yeah, he might be angry at his mother for a long time, but I could tell he loved her anyway, even though she'd spent most of his life encouraging him toward callousness.

"Blaine Harcourt, you have the biggest heart in the world." I looked up at him until he met my gaze. His eyes shone with emotions too numerous to catalog.

"Congratulations. It belongs to you, Kimiko Ichiro."

He demonstrated, and I began paying him back for such a generous gift. I had the feeling it'd take a lifetime to equal it. After a while, we slept.

CHAPTER EIGHTEEN

Blaine

I didn't fly us into Newport. Dragon shifter Mourning Days lasted twenty-four hours, during which we couldn't eat or sleep. The last thing I needed was to be starved as well as exhausted. I sat in the back of the unmarked sedan Josh had borrowed from his parents with my arm around Kimiko. Her breath was light and even, telling me she dozed most of the way over. Nox elbowed him, not exactly distracting him from driving as she pointed out my public display of affection for the woman who'd broken vault security but spared my heart the same fate. I leaned my head against hers as Josh pulled the car into the long driveway.

"So, they're going to arrest me inside, then, I take it."

"No one's getting arrested, you big paranoid lunk."

"But Detective Weaver tried it last night."

"Detective Weaver was mistaken. The evidence supported your story."

"How'd she get that kind of evidence?"

"You taking off like that apparently put out the cat signal."

"You mean I have Hinky Neighborhood Cat-man to thank for not being in jail during my stepfather's Mourning Day?"

"That's pretty much the size of it, yeah."

No Newport PD vehicles guarded the entrance. All I saw was an unmarked one pulling away with Tony Gitano in the back and Detective Weaver driving. He looked tired, not angry or scared to be in the back of a cruiser like that. I wondered why he wasn't in the front if he'd been helping the police. Then I remembered. The Gatto Gang were all Italian shifters from Federal Hill in Providence, mostly big cats like lions and panthers. Tony might ride in the back so he wouldn't look like a rat. All the same, I was pissed that I owed my freedom to a wannabe vigilante who turned into a fluffy little kitty cat.

Kimiko woke up and covered my mouth before I could get around to colorful metaphors about Tony Gitano in English. I continued rattling off words in Italian, Spanish, French, Latin, Greek, waiting to see whether she'd catch the fact that I'd switched to terms of endearment about her. Judging by the blushing smile, she did. I gazed down at her, memorizing the exact color of her cheeks, the arc of her smile, the feel of her palm against my lips. I'd need to keep my mind on all of that if I expected to get through this day alongside Mother.

We got out of the car and headed down the path to the back where everything would be set up. There would be two crystal urns, one for Mother and the other for me. Mourning Day couldn't happen inside, at least not for Mother and me or any other dragonish guests. And when I rounded the corner, I saw that almost everyone was there for her. I took a deep breath and turned right, so the cliff walk was on my left. A salt-tinged breeze blew what remained of my hair flat against my skull when I approached the transparent containers where each guest would leave something behind, a literal paying of respects. I stepped beside the one with my name engraved on it and dropped my item in.

The clink of the lucite keepsake locket one important woman had given me attracted the attention of the other. When Mother looked up and saw what I'd done and how I'd paid, her nostrils flared, and she actually put a hand to her lips. She stopped just short of touching them, though. Of course, she wouldn't want to smudge that blood-red lipstick. Everything was about appearances for her. I'd cut that line of thinking off with my hair that morning.

I didn't avert my gaze even though the color of the paint on her lips had inspired a stream of smoke to rise above me. And I rose above my anger, forgave her in my heart even if I couldn't say the words that day. Forgiving Mother wasn't about her. It wasn't even about Wilfred. It was about me, and my sibling, who slept in the egg below the mansion. Kimiko had been right. My heart was big, more vast than I'd imagined. And it was like the sea I'd grown up alongside, prone to both calm and tempest. It was up to me to decide whether to be still or surge. I'd decided to reserve the latter for enemies only. Today, I'd be surrounded by friends.

"Nice haircut, Blaine." Lynn Frampton didn't sound sarcastic, for once. She placed a blue and white handkerchief in my urn.

"Um, thanks, I think?"

"Someone had to make up for the stink-eye over there." The human girl who'd probably beat my GPA this semester shrugged. Lynn was smart but not always wise. Still, she knew tons about dealing with people disliking her. "You look dapper. I mean that."

I nodded, then faked a wince as Bobby Tremain, Lynn's mate and my roommate, punched me in the arm.

"Sorry about all this, dragon-man."

"Thanks, Bobby."

"No, I mean it. We should have been here." Bobby dropped a

whittled carving of a bear in. I could tell by its style he'd done it himself.

"No way, man." I ran my hand over my head, coming up short, just like my hair. "I let you all think Trogdor could handle burninating everything on his own."

"Yeah, well, I definitely should have known better." Josh paid his respects with a tin wolf figurine. Nox clung to his arm, adding an obsidian arrowhead after it.

"Don't beat yourself up, Dennison." I glanced over my shoulder at the unexpected voice. Fred Redford tipped his hat at me. No one cared that his Paw Sox cap was completely out of place at a Mourning Day. Redcaps and their Changeling kin literally couldn't go anywhere without their hats. "I should have known he'd need help, too. And I was just on the other side of a little water." He put a pin with the Pawtucket Red Sox logo on it into the urn.

"Hey, can we stop with the whole Worst Friend contest? I had help anyway." I gave Kimiko's hand a squeeze. "The important thing is, you're here now. Thanks, you guys. I've got to shift and get in place before the dirge starts."

"Hey, call me anytime you need to today." Kimiko tapped her right temple, then pressed her lips close to my ear. "You don't have to do this alone," she whispered.

I spent the rest of the day perched on the second-highest gable on the mansion. Through our psychic link, Kimiko let part of my heart and mind rest in our shared mindscape glade. She also showed me the fanfare surrounding the Sidhe Queen's arrival. She had one of her courtiers with her, another Sidhe Lady with her matching son Al in tow. I remembered him from a Fall semester class. He paid his respects by dropping a copper wire sculpture of a dragon into the urn. Kimiko let me hear Al's expression of sympathy and its unexpected sincerity resonated with the musical keening I had to maintain for the entire Mourning Day. I barely knew the kid, his mom was a peripheral friend of Mothers, and yet he'd still thought to bring something for me. I'd never forget that.

After sunset, I couldn't greet Henry and Maddie in person. Kimiko did it for me. Henry, who knew what it was like to lose someone close enough to be family, let his actions speak. He was a memory psychic, not a poet, after all. He pressed an old cassette tape labeled "marriage mix" into my mate's hand before adding it to the urn. Kimiko and I watched a memory snippet of Wilfred and Mother dancing to Billy Idol's White Wedding at Henrietta Thurston's reception. Maddie added a clear paperweight which I happened to know used to be the anchor for a Grim.

And then, Olivia Adler showed up. The owl shifter wore light blue to honor the element she shared with Wilfred. I'd almost forgotten he'd tutored her in Practical Flight last semester. Her wardrobe choice made her stick out so much I noticed from the roof. She had Jeannie La Montagne with her, which I thought was a big surprise until I saw what she carried. A brass lamp, old fashioned and tinged green with tarnish almost everywhere. Through Kimiko, I smelled seawater.

My mate kept me from listening in, telling me that some things Jeannie had to say weren't her secrets to tell. What she did let me see was Olivia leaving a white tail feather, its tip honed into a quill and shimmering like an opal. Jeannie dropped in what looked like the promise ring I'd seen her take off the night of the drive-by shooting.

I almost stopped my keening when the Djinn popped out of the lamp. Kimiko called him Ismail and thanked him for coming. He also put a ring into the urn, although his looked like an antique of Turkish design. Kimiko didn't let Ismail apologize. She and I both agreed that none of what had happened was his fault. He'd done the best he could under the circumstances.

I knew dawn was close even before Henry left. The sun tinged the eastern sky, signaling to the dragons on the roof that we could stop our keening and come down now. A glamour screen left behind by the Sidhe Queen gave us cover to dress after we shifted back to our human forms. I waited for Mother to say something, but she didn't. Neither did Taki Waban. I noticed they didn't talk to each other, either. Didn't even exchange glances. Once dressed, I walked away, leaving them to their strangely avoidant behavior.

Crossing the lawn to Kimiko was like coming home, even though I strode away from the house I'd grown up in. Josh's car was still in the driveway since he and Nox had fallen asleep inside it while waiting for us. When we got in, they woke up, and Josh started the car. About halfway back to Providence, Kimiko cleared her throat.

"So, that wasn't awkward at all."

I chuckled, and something broke in my chest. I shouldn't say that. It was as though all the pain that went with caring too much about the wrong people had gone out with the Mourning Day keening. That thing in my chest was love. It hadn't broken. Instead, it had hatched.

EDWARD REDFORD AND THE SINISTER SPINDLE

**A Providence Paranormal College
Short Story**

EDWARD REDFORD AND THE SINISTER SPINDLE

Robert

Whenever Ed Redford came home from school, I made myself invisible. I knew what he was in for, how his life wouldn't have a normal span or a normal anything for that matter. And I hadn't needed a Precognitive Psychic to tell me so, either.

Ghosts like me, especially those of us haunting around for long enough to see a dozen generations born, then die and sometimes unlive, find patterns the Extrahumans don't. Mortality is limiting; everyone knows that, even the vampires and the Fae who live much longer than most. But they're still more limited than a ghost like me with a long memory. Solidity has a grounding effect that persists through the first few decades for most ghosts.

I'm not most ghosts.

I'll introduce myself to you the same way I did young Edward, even though he couldn't understand or speak any human language when he became my Medium. My name is Robert

Crandall Lafayette the Second. The boy calls me Rob, but I only allow that because he will be the most powerful Psychic Medium since I was a solid. That was hundreds of years ago.

The boy was only five days old when he stopped breathing in his bassinet. He technically died for a moment through no fault of his own, but recovered due to the speedy response of a medical team. That's how we met. And no, it's none of your business why infant Edward stopped breathing. That tale is his to spin for you or not, as he chooses.

His mother Delilah is a Medium too, but I wanted nothing to do with her. My loyalty is to his patriarchal side, the Redfords, who contracted me to serve their family after one of them avenged my unfortunate demise at the Roanoke Colony. No, I won't tell you about it. The entire debacle is part of the government's Classified Extrahuman History files, and you haven't got the proper clearance levels for that.

I agreed to discuss young Edward Redford's strange discovery with you, however, so that's the focus for now. We spend a typical afternoon together thusly: the boy arrives home and tries to scrounge a snack amidst his lunkish Redcap brother's and father's near-constant feasting. I don't help him. I pretend this is a way of training him to be more assertive, but it's actually due to the fact that his mother has a veritable army of ghosts at her command, all devoting themselves to the task of conveying anything edible from the kitchen to the hungry Redcaps' gullets. Even a ghost of my age and potency isn't much good at bypassing that many of the more lowbrow variety. Working against their efforts is like trying to swim up a waterfall.

Once Edward has something resembling a snack, I follow him up to his attic bedroom and then down into the basement where he procrastinates on his homework by practicing Mediumship with me. This has always been our little secret, mostly because none of the other Redfords bother with the back stairs. Delilah Redford's ghosts use it as a sort of refuge, but they and the boy don't mind sharing it. Edward's family doesn't check on him in his room until at least an hour after the Redcap feeding frenzy ends.

On that particular afternoon, our practice focused on identifying items imbued with Psychic energy. I'd been down in the basement during the wee hours of the morning, memorizing the locations of any such thing in preparation. But Edward honed his attention to pinpoint one box in the corner by the root cellar, something that hadn't been there before. I let him pull the dusty drop cloth off its top and fold open the lid. But when I saw the item within, I couldn't stand by any longer.

"Stop," I said. "Step away from that box immediately."

"Okay, Rob." The boy did as he was told. He'd never been obviously willful, just quietly rebellious. And rarely against me in any event. "Is that thing bad news?"

"I believe it might be, though I'll need a closer look to be certain."

Floating over to the cardboard crate was easy, too much so, in fact. But that only confirmed my suspicions.

"That's a Soul Spindle in the box. It's extremely dangerous to anything incorporeal."

"So, ghosts and out-of-body Psychics?"

"Yes, and technically will-o'-the-wisps, although only the ones who have left the Under."

"Yeah." Ed shrugged. "I don't know much about the Under."

"Oh, worry not." As I mentioned, I am aware of many things my young protégé is not. "You'll learn it all exceedingly well someday."

"So, aren't devices like Soul Spindles supposed to be registered, with slips on file and everything?"

"You are correct." I floated away from it, a task that took more of my energy than getting there in the first place. "I want you to go back over there and close the box, then cover it up as close to the way you found it as possible. But before you do that, look inside and see what if anything, is in there with the thrice-accursed device. And don't touch it, mind."

Edward peered in at the thing, his lips twisting in that way I knew meant something both upset and intrigued him. He folded the flaps back over the Soul Spindle in the reverse order he'd opened them and then draped the cloth. It wasn't precisely the same, but in such a way that a mouse might have disturbed it instead of a curious boy.

"There was a slip in the box, Rob, but it didn't look right. There wasn't a seal like you see on a legally approved one."

"Then it's as I suspected."

"What?"

"You're a smart boy, smarter than that potty wizard in those fanciful tomes you read after lights out." He indubitably was, which was why I always spoke to him like an adult. He'd have to grow up fast. "Why don't you tell me what you can deduce about this highly regulated item hiding in your parents' basement?"

"Well, if the slip isn't approved, then maybe it hasn't changed hands since before the Reveal. Mom might be selling it."

"In all the time we've been coming down here, have you noticed that box in the corner before now?"

"No." The line I knew would become a constant feature on Edward's face in his later years grew between his eyebrows. "So it's a black market item. Whoever put it here is hiding it until they can get the slip embossed to make it look legit."

"Precisely the conclusion I made. Excellent work." I floated over to the door to the back stairs. "Now, we ought to postpone our lessons for today. Or perhaps longer. Until the box is gone in any event."

"I get it." The boy paced quietly toward me. "We steer clear because whoever puts the fake seal on that slip will come down here, and we don't want to tangle with shady characters. Because I'm too young to be a proper ghost like you, Rob."

"Exactly."

Edward didn't speak again until we got back up to his room. "I can't figure out whose it is, though."

"No?" It was my turn to let my thoughts run rampant.

It had been so long since I'd been a small mortal child, it would take a few minutes to put myself in Edward's place, during which he'd continue to sulk. Rather than observe that, I drifted into the wall, hovering in my favorite thinking spot behind the portrait everyone but the boy thought was of me.

The boy wouldn't want to believe the simplest explanation that the illegal Soul Spindle in the basement belonged to his parents. He also wouldn't want to let his mind make the next leap, to the conclusion that one or both were involved in some criminal enterprise.

Edward's father had a somewhat public history of doing magical contract work on buildings owned by the local mafia Boss, Gino Gitano. But that had been years ago before even Ed's college-age brother was born. Neil Redford had taken strictly legitimate jobs at the first sign there'd be a Great Reveal, abandoning Gino as a business contact.

That left the boy's mother, Delilah. But his parentally dominated brain came to a roundabout conclusion I hadn't anticipated.

"It's gotta be Fred."

At the sound of his voice, I stuck my head back through the wall. Edward flopped on his bed, staring at the ceiling.

"How?"

"Fred's been hanging out more with Tony Gitano ever since they went to PPC together." The boy sat up. "I bet Tony stole that thing from his dad and hid it here."

"Why would Tony do that?"

"I don't know. Because everyone thinks he's hinky?"

"What I meant to ask was, why would Tony Gitano jeopardize his scholarship over an item he can't even legitimize in order to sell?"

"Hormones?"

"Those don't work quite the way you think, Ed. It's not your brother or Tony. Neither of them can sense Psychic energies in any case. And I have it on the best authority that Gino does his son Tony no favors." I had, in fact, witnessed this myself on more than one occasion, but a full account would have frightened the boy out of his wits, so I refrained from relating it.

"Okay." The boy leaned forward, hanging his head. "It's Mom, then. She's Psychic and can actually use the thing. Didn't Mediums use them to get rid of Wraiths back before the Reveal?"

"Once upon a time, Ed, they did. But Soul Spindles are restricted magipsychic devices now. We discussed this before. Do you remember why?"

"Only government-employed Mediums can use them, checked out from a Federal bank for each instance of Wraith removal. It's because the Spindles also hurt Projecting Psychics."

"Right. So why is an illegal Soul Spindle in your house?"

"It can't be because Mom needs a Wraith removed. There aren't any here, and the FBE comes within twenty-four hours on Wraith calls. She's called them before."

"So what does that imply?"

"My mom has a beef with a Projecting Psychic."

"Bingo."

"But why?"

"That's a mystery we lack clues to solve. But I'm sure more will reveal themselves in time."

"Okay."

After that, the boy actually pulled his schoolwork out of his knapsack and worked on it. Even mathematics. I could hardly blame him after the hard truths he'd just had to face.

I felt no guilt, only a vague sense of pride. Edward would go through worse than this soon. After that day, I had hope that he could handle what was to come. An auspicious conclusion on my part because he'd have to do it all without me.

The series continues with *Djinn and Bear It coming May 27, 2021.*

CONNECT WITH THE AUTHOR

Find D.R. Perry Online

Website: https://drperryauthor.com/

Author Central: http://www.amazon.com/-/e/B00O6851HO

Facebook: https://www.facebook.com/drpperry/

Mailing List: https://app.mailerlite.com/webforms/
landing/p9i8u6

Twitter: https://twitter.com/DRPerry22

www.ingramcontent.com/pod-product-compliance
Lightning Source LLC
Chambersburg PA
CBHW050413110726
47899CB00008B/2702